Lost Now Here

Phoebe Garnsworthy

Also by Phoebe Garnsworthy:

Lost Nowhere: A Journey of Self-Discovery (Book 1 of 2)

Daily Rituals: Positive Affirmations to Attract Love, Happiness and Peace

The Spirit Guides: A Coming-of-Age Novella

Define Me / Divine Me : A Poetic Display of Affection

Copyright © 2018 by **Phoebe Garnsworthy**
Lost Now Here -- 1st ed.
ISBN-978-0-9954119-5-1

Artwork by Durian Addict

www.PhoebeGarnsworthy.com

Dedication

This book is dedicated to the Eternal Soul within us.

To the Divine Light that shines through our being, spreading love and warmth to the world around us.

Our journey together is never-ending, constantly learning, unlearning, and relearning.

Acknowledgement

For my love, Adrien.

Contents

Astral Dreaming 1

Igniting the Witch Within 14

The Arrival 19

Tattoo Faces 25

Praza, the 2nd Land 33

Fishing 46

Three Full Moons 53

The Pilgrimage 64

Parietal Art 77

Xous — the Underworld 81

Tehar and Mia Veol 91

King Devya of Deia 106

A Journey to the Middle World 113

The Blessing 126

The Power of One 133

Connected by Love 141

The Wise Old Oak Tree 148

The Najatinis 156

The Land of Salor 169

The Truth 172

Death Moon 182

Ancestors 197

In the Dreamtime 203

About the Author 207

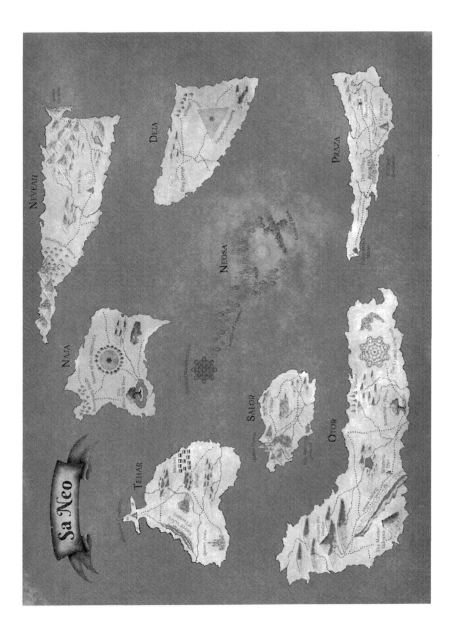

one

Astral Dreaming

Lily walked along the crystal-pebbled beach and listened to the sounds of the waves as they swept against the soles of her feet. As the water licked around her ankles, she felt as though the waves were soothing their own desires to feel something different just as much as she was: a yearning for change. She closed her eyes with intense pleasure, breathing slowly as she connected with a force that felt so radiantly alive. She looked to the ground to see what land she had arrived upon, but the crystals shone so brightly they blinded her vision. It was as though the sun had pierced the crystals skin and stolen all color from the world to see.

Lily continued along the beach until she reached the opening of a small cave. It was tiny—a miniature little hole that only she could crawl through—but she knew she had to go inside. A voice in her heart was commanding her forward. And so, on hands and knees she crawled through the space.

Inside the air was moist, and the crystals were cold on her bare feet. She could hear the soft trickling of water in the far distance; it was the sound of the ocean tiptoeing through the cave. From above, small slivers of light shone through, illuminating her pathway and displaying another opening in front of her. This second opening dropped straight down, and a staircase spiraled around in a circle, with each step organically carved out, inviting Lily to walk down.

Large slabs of moss grew over the stones, but not the slimy kind you could fall on—it supported and protected her, and it comforted her feet like a plush carpet, encouraging her to continue on her journey. Step by step, Lily continued down. The humidity in the air around her felt sticky on her skin, but she wasn't scared and to keep her mind busy she focused on her breathing as she walked, noticing the way her body relaxed as she did so. She hummed lightly, a song that used to calm her when she was a child.

"Everything …is going to be okay …everything is going …to be all right …"

With each step down she chanted, and with each step her eyes adjusted to the darkness. One step down, breathe in, "everything," two steps down, breathe out, "is going to be okay."

She arrived at the base of the stairwell and in this space the darkness completely engulfed her vision. But as she turned to the right, she saw a brilliant light shining in front of her. It was a ceiling of glowing crystals that hung low above her head and shone in sparkling patterns against the cave walls. Lily followed the lights until it brought her to a small pool of water that opened directly below. She stood on the edge of the rocks and peered down. A desire to dive deep into the unknown was tugging on the edges of her thoughts. A daredevil idea of whether the pool of water reached the ocean's edge, or whether it was a trap, a hole of empty promises and broken dreams, a false reality destined to conceal her fate forever. She wondered if both options would give her the sense of freedom she desired. Both ideas escaped her current reality regardless of the outcome. If she were to make it to the ocean, perhaps she would see her mermaid friends once more, who she missed so terribly. And if instead she continued to swim until her very last breath, unable to be free, perhaps the afterlife was freedom in itself. Providing her with the answers of life's questions she terribly wanted to know. Lily contemplated her ideas as she listened to the sounds of the water as it purred in soft ripples, whispering stories to her ears.

Small droplets of water dripped down from the ceiling above and as they fell into the water below, they painted a light waterfall in harmonious chimes. Each droplet sounded sweeter than the last, and each took its time, gracefully allowing each other to sing their own song. The musical rainfall tantalized her ears, and she thought, if twinkling stars were to make a sound, this is what it would be. Lily kneeled to the edge of the water to stare at her reflection. She had been a small child of 12 when she first visited Sa Neo, and now her face was that of a 15-year-old. Her eyes were still the same, green hues framed with slivers of black; the darkness hinted at her deeply held emotions, despite her innocence. Her hair, a careless mess of light-brown curls, now grew wild and more luscious. She smiled. It had taken her a long time to like the face she saw smiling back at her, but here she was, three years later and so happy. She was so content with this acceptance of herself and most importantly, she was now finally open to new beginnings.

Suddenly, the reflection in the water changed into a dark-black swirl. There was something in the water below. In one quick motion, a young man leapt from the water and hovered above as soft waves lapped at his chest. He spoke no words and stole the voice from Lily's own chest. With captivating eyes that matched the darkness in the ocean, a deep blue-black, he just stared at her. Lily longed to find herself within the depths of his eyes, wondering if he held the answers to what it was that she would seek. And so she stared, mesmerized by the man's appearance. His jawline was strong, and his body mirrored that of strength with defined muscles.

Neither said a word. Both she and the young man stared, as though their eyes were magnetically drawn to each other. A calling from within their Soul, a longing to learn more. Lily felt a strange hypnotic pull like never before. From her heart to his heart connected a long silver cord that flickered; it appeared and disappeared as fast as a lightning bolt. Proving that the connection was not only felt, it was real. Lily shyly looked away. The young man held little expression on his face, but his eyes, his eyes looked at her in a way she had never been looked at before. She felt as though the memory of his eyes had been stained into her mind from many lifetimes ago.

"I've been looking for you," he said as he pointed to the necklace that hung on his chest.

It was the same Ouroboros charm necklace that dangled around hers. An identical match, even the black and white eyes were the same. A white and a black pearl, perfectly opposite and yet desperately needed to define one another.

"Have you?" Lily asked.

"Yes," he said as he held out his hand. "It's me, Indigo."

A warm flow of energy moved through the air from the base of his hand and it danced around where she stood. She lifted her hand in response, moving closer to the handsome merman. Her hand touched his hand. The complex opposites of wet to dry, warm to cold balanced each other in harmony. And a current of electricity bolted through the both of them so fiercely and so strong that it ignited a blazing spark within the entire room, forcefully blowing the two apart.

Lily was thrown against the floor, and she opened her eyes faintly, seeing a blur of Indigo now stretched out in front of her. He pushed half his body on the edge of the rocks and opened his mouth in slow motion.

"Help us!" Indigo pleaded as the rocks lifted up and swallowed him whole, crushing his body to sink below the water.

"Indigo!" Lily screamed as she opened her eyes and jolted upright.

She was sitting safely back home in her own bed. The sound of the rain strummed against the window; it was falling heavily from the clouds with no sun to warm up the new day. She had dreamed about traveling to Sa Neo again. The same dream had haunted her many times even though it had been years since she had visited. Yet, she had never returned.

Why? she asked herself.

The temptation to explore was always inside her, but she quietened that voice, too fearful of what she had done. The images of those tortured Souls had never disappeared from her mind. The memory of what had been, and the emotions of fear, regret and anguish still felt as real as if she had felt them moments ago. She had been carrying the weight of her past on her shoulders, and to revisit what she had done terrified Lily the most.

To some extent she had moved on with her life. She was earning good grades at school and was completely off the medication. She still didn't have any friends, but it didn't matter—because she loved herself. She focused on improving herself, on expanding her mind with knowledge, and doing the things that made her happy. Yet, she still felt like there was something missing. Something lingered inside her wanting to get out. A question of reality, perhaps? Of whether the fantasy world that she traveled to really did exist. But then she kept telling herself that it was nonsense. That she found the gifts from the "World of Sa Neo" right underneath the house when she explored. That "nothing was real." It was easier that way.

Lily sat down at her nightstand and opened up the drawers which held the secrets from the past. A magic scroll of spells, seven crystals, and little potions from the lands. The initiation ring sparkled unusually bright. It was a deep purple amethyst with frosted edges of white. She placed it on her finger and immediately felt a pulse of energy. Her fingers straightened uncontrollably, and her hand started to shake. She covered the ring with her other hand, trying to control the energy. But it was too strong, and she felt dizzy. Lily took it off quickly, immediately regaining consciousness. She looked at herself in the mirror as she touched the Ouroboros charm necklace that she still wore fastened around her neck. The edges of gold that caressed the skin of the serpent were now worn with age.

But the eyes still shone brightly, one black, one white. The last gift from her mermaid friends.

Lily had never told anyone about her secret place. And why would she? No one would understand and if she tried to explain it she knew it would mean that she would have to go see the doctors again. Even though deep down she believed that she didn't imagine it. She couldn't have. Her whole personality changed overnight from visiting the world of Sa Neo. She had woken up and realized how strong her mind could be, how powerful she really was. She was responsible for creating the world around her to be as beautiful as she wanted it to be.

Then there were the gifts from the land—the ring, the magic scroll of spells. How could any of that be explained? How was it that she could bring into her reality something tangible from her imagination? She had shifted places, shifted universes in a matter of a split second. No one needed to know. No one. It would be her little secret.

Lily got dressed into her favorite floral dress and walked to the living area to see if her father was awake. He was sitting on the maroon sofa, reading the newspaper and combing his mustache with a pointed finger. A strong cup of coffee sat on the table next to him; the aroma drifted through the space as she joined him.

"Good morning, Papa," Lily said, as she kissed him lightly on the cheek.

He patted her elbow while she did so, with a big smile across his face.

"How did you sleep, my darling?" he asked as he folded his newspaper and placed it on the chair.

"Okay. I'm just happy that it's Saturday, I want to play in the garden," she replied as she walked through the colorful glass doors that led to the veranda.

Lily hung on the edge of the balcony as she looked over the fence. The enchantment of the garden was calling her name. The leaves of the bushes danced hurriedly amongst the wind, and the branches of the shrubs that lined up perfectly in a row were swaying back and forth from the great gushing of the rainfall. But the rain didn't deter her, it only made her more excited. If the leaves and the trees were dancing so joyously, she would too.

"Lily, you can't go outside, you'll catch a cold. It's far too wet and there's a very strong breeze," her father said as he joined her on the veranda. "Practice your piano playing for a while instead and I'll bring you some warm tea with ginger biscuits, now how does that sound?"

Lily turned to frown at her father and looked back toward the garden. She peered over the edge of the veranda down below to the deep terra-cotta-colored tiles. Small puddles had begun to form, and they reflected up towards her, mirroring the sky, the heavy clouds, and her own face. Colorful lizards and beetles drank lavishly from the puddles; they looked like they were having such a grand time swimming in the shallow water. Lily longed to join the party, and she sighed with disappointment, imagining that everyone was having fun except for her.

Father patted Lily's hair lovingly and then tugged her lightly by the shoulders.

"Come now, Lily, it's far too cold to stand outside today."

"But, Father." Lily placed her hand on the stone veranda. It was freezing cold as Father had warned, and she felt like she had put her hand on top of the icebox in the kitchen. But she needed to feel the stirring of nature one last time before she went inside. And felt it she did, as the heavy droplets of rain pierced down onto her hands hurriedly with thick splotches. They shot down hard like arrows, a light stinging sensation on her skin. Lily didn't mind the pain though, it was a change of sensation and to her it was exciting.

"Come on now, Lily," her father pleaded again, this time with a bit more force as he guided her inside.

But as Lily walked back inside she stared at the veranda, watching the rain one last time and hearing the wind blow strongly through the trees. She could have sworn that she had heard the trees whispering to her. They kept saying, "Come join us, Lily. Come outside and play."

"Do an hour of practice on the piano, my darling, and then, if the rain has stopped, you can go outside, okay?" Father said as he patted Lily's hand and took hold of it, directing her back inside the house.

Lily looked behind once more at the sky. The clouds had changed shape drastically. The edges of them had now formed a puffy pillow, as though smoke had blown from a fire and filled it up like a giant balloon.

Such marvelous shapes, she thought. And she wondered how it was that the clouds looked like they could be landed on, yet in reality they were so transparent as though nothing existed at all. They moved hurriedly with the wind, swirling in patterns, changing shapes and sizes and gliding in one direction. She felt as though they were talking to her, telling her which way to come. *Soon,* she thought. *I will join you soon.* As though satisfied with the response, they twirled in a circle on the spot, dancing with glee, as though they were performing just for her.

Inside the house felt cozy. An open fire was lit on the side wall of the living room and it had warmed up the whole house. Lily sat on the carpet in between the sofa and the fire. The carpet had a black-and-cream pattern of a labyrinth; it reminded Lily of a game. She pulled out a wooden angel figurine from her pocket and played with it along the lines, moving it up and down through the maze as though exploring its own land. The sound of the water outside splashed down harder and Lily looked up, watching the droplets of water slither down the window like snakes chasing each other. She moved closer to the fire, feeling the warmth cushion her body with a nurturing sensation. She listened to the fire crackle as it burned with brilliance and breathed energy into the air above. But she didn't just like to watch the flames caress the wood; no, she loved to see the things that no one else bothered to watch. The way the coal would glisten from the fire, how it would change its own shape so that it could mold into something new. The dancing shadows in the background fascinated her. She wondered how such darkness could be created from something so beautiful.

The magic of the fire reminded her of the witches in Sa Neo and the ceremonies that would take place around the fire in the woods. She closed her eyes and imagined what kind of rituals might be playing out. The sound of crackling fire was even more thrilling when she couldn't see it. She loved to listen to the miniature explosions that erupted from the wood as it crumbled beneath the pressure of the heat. Between the sounds of the wood burning and the heavy rainfall outside, Lily felt enveloped between a split chaos of madness. Which would she prefer, she wondered. Drenched in the freezing cold with endless splinters of water gushing over her head, her skin, and her body? Or boiling hot from the fire, with boils and burns from a scalding heat? She jumped between the two ideas and wriggled uneasily.

"What are you doing Lily?" Father asked as he brought her favorite dandelion tea and little round-shaped ginger biscuits to her.

"Oh Papa, I was trying to figure out what I'd rather be, freezing cold or boiling hot. If you had to pick one? If you had to!" Lily asked, jumping up to help her father with the silver tray.

Father placed the tray down on the center table and lifted up the teapot to pour it into a green-painted cup.

"Lily, you are funny. That's a question that your mother would have asked!" He winked.

"Really, Papa?" Lily loved hearing stories about her mother; although she had made peace with her passing, the feeling of not knowing who she really was presented itself to Lily time and time again, and Lily cherished those words of encouragement more than her father knew.

"Yes, you are growing more and more like her every day." Father smiled, and Lily felt as though he could see her late mother in her.

"Okay, hmm …I think maybe I'd like to be cold; yes, cold is my choice," he smiled soothingly, as his mustache curled to the side of his face near his cheeks.

"Ah …to be cold all day," Lily shivered as she imagined herself surrounded by ice-cold winds, snowy mountains, and constant rain.

"And you?" Father asked, as he too took a ginger biscuit and sat back down on the maroon sofa.

"Well, if it has to be one or the other …" Lily shook her head, disappointed with the two choices, although knowing perfectly well that she was the one who originated the idea.

"I think I would rather be too hot. At least if I died I would feel a nice soothing sensation of warmth and heat," Lily concluded as she picked up a ginger biscuit and took a big bite, feeling the sweet sugars crumble in her mouth.

"If you died?" Father opened his mouth wide with a slight shock of horror.

Lily couldn't help but giggle at the way his lips wavered. She noticed the pointed tips of his mustache move unevenly, as though they each held their own identity and agreed and disagreed with his reaction.

"Yes, Father!" Lily half winked as she smiled smugly to herself. "If I died, I would like to be nice and warm and cuddly instead of frozen. The oven is much nicer than the icebox!"

"So, you prefer to watch the fire than build snowmen?" Father chuckled to himself, knowing very well that Lily would much rather be playing with the snow. And as expected, Lily's face turned sour with the disappointment of having made the wrong choice.

"Well ..."

"Now, now. You've made your decision," her father teased.

Lily stood up and moved back to the windows that looked out to the veranda; faintly through the glass she could see the furthermost tree where a thick stream of smoke moved in the air and upward. *Witches!* she thought, and she opened up the door hurriedly to get a better look. Lily ran to the edge of the veranda and peered down below at the smoke, but the rain was too strong, and the winds were too fierce; it was impossible to see anything. The clouds had now turned into a thick grey blanket; it covered the sky like a mist, concealing any existence of her backyard. As a shot of lightning hit the sky an electrifying sensation shot up through Lily's body. She had never felt anything quite like it. But instead of the lightning shooting back down to the ground to disappear, it stood strong to the ground and it didn't move. A thick zigzag of lightning had mystically appeared between the sky and the ground and had landed directly in front of Lily's eyes. Her mouth gaped open with astonishment, and she wondered whether she had paused in time. How was it that such a phenomenon could occur? She wanted to call to Father, but she didn't want to turn away. Her eyes were glued to the bolt of lightning that split the sky in two and directed her gaze down to the ground. As though something was holding it there. The rain around her grew louder, while soft hues in the sky quivered. Light then dark, and light then dark. Still that lightning bolt didn't move.

SMASH!

The door slammed loudly behind her, too loudly. And she looked behind to see a thick crack in the glass window of the door.

"Lily!" she heard her father yell.

Lily looked back to the lightning bolt, but it had now disappeared, and she reluctantly walked back inside to face the blame from Father.

"I'm sorry," Lily said timidly as she walked back inside the house with a big frown on her face. "It was an accident, really."

"I know it was darling, but I told you not to play outside, it's far too cold and windy," Father said as he shook his head and stood up to look at the crack in the door. "Now what about that piano?"

"Yes, Papa, okay, I will practice," Lily replied as she went back downstairs to the piano room.

Lily sat on the yellow chair while she sang sweet melodies through her fingertips. Each strumming heartbeat that moved through the instrument created such a beautiful sound. She imagined each chord that moved through the piano was a little piece of energy, an actual living thing, and as it was released, it felt a great relief, singing a tune while doing so, being thankful for being released back into the atmosphere. Lily liked to think about energy. The way it was constantly moving and changing. It was her favorite subject at school, in her science class. And she often would study for extra-long hours, learning about the universe and planets. It was the only thing she wanted to learn more about because it was her best opportunity to find out if the world of Sa Neo was real.

It's so silly. *Why don't I try to visit it again?* Lily asked herself as she continued to play the piano. Even though the idea of seeing Sa Neo and all her friends delighted her greatly, there was still a heavy weight of sadness inside of her. The feeling of regret haunted her. Whether her actions did more harm than good, and would she even be welcomed back? Or did they blame her for bringing change to their world? Were her friends okay? Was everyone safe? Happy? And then there were the dreams. Too many dreams to count. A calling for her to return there. As the music continued to play through her fingers, an idea took over her thoughts. The idea to return to Sa Neo. Today was the day. She had decided. The weather had restricted her to play inside and she had done all her homework. There was nothing else left to do.

two

Igniting the Witch Within

Lily went back to her bedroom to collect a small pouch and fill it with the right tools to navigate through the world safely. She opened the drawer to her dresser and picked up the pieces from her visit before. Seven colored crystals, one color to represent each land that she could travel to. As she placed the crystals in her pouch, she reminisced about the five lands she had already visited and the two lands she had yet to explore.

The first land, Otor, had the red garnet crystals. Lily felt a calming sensation when thinking of the land of Otor and all her friends. She wondered how Jacques was in his pointed pyramid, and how Karisma was in her great big treehouse. She smiled to herself as she thought about it, she missed them both very much. The third land, Salor, had the yellow citrine crystals and although she only visited it for a short time, it still held great meaning for her and she wondered if Silvia ever escaped to find her family. Tehar was the fourth land, although Lily shuddered with remembrance as she touched the green malachite crystal. The green crystal in Lily's hand represented oppression, a land full of people who hated their ruler, and wanted nothing more than to be set free. She wondered if justice was ever delivered. The fifth land, Deia with the blue kyanite crystals, was next, and again, Lily felt nervous thinking about it. How lucky she was to have had Karisma by her side when she visited. And lastly, she picked up the purple amethyst, the seventh land, called Neveah. The greatest mystical land of them all. With the most powerful empress she had ever met, Violetta. As she remembered, Lily felt as though Neveah was the most surreal of them all. With reflective creatures and floating lands, did Neveah even exist at all?

There were only two lands that Lily hadn't visited: the second land, full of orange carnelian crystals, and the sixth land, which was covered in dark blue azurite. The crystals knocked each other as they fell into her pouch, and she wondered if they felt the same as she did, nervous and excited for an adventure ahead. Lily picked up the initiation ring again but this time she didn't put it on her finger, terrified that the power would be too strong in her world. The box that held the scroll of magic spells was next, and Lily opened the box, pulling out the scroll and staring at the empty pages. *So strange that the magic doesn't work here,* Lily thought. Nonetheless, she placed it inside the pouch. Now, for the gifts. The world of Sa Neo relied on the act of giving gifts. It was an exchange of energy, a way to show gratitude for sharing someone's time. Lily searched through the drawers of her dressing table to collect some special things that she could give: little shells from the seaside, a twig of rosemary from the garden, a butterfly cocoon, a feather from a white dove, a dried brown acorn, an antique key, and a string of beads that she had found on the side of the street one day.

With a packed bag full of treasures, Lily climbed down beneath the house to try to recreate the same scenario from before. She opened the trapdoor to the cellar below the wooden floor and threw down a stepladder. She was taller now and would have no problem getting out. The ground felt drier than last time; the mud had now sealed to a crackly surface of a cake-like matter. A small part of her was tempted to get some water and make mud pies with it. The texture of the dirt was too inviting to leave alone. *No,* she heard a voice inside her say, *it's time to move on.* Lily closed her eyes, waiting to see the crystal light shining from within to guide her on the journey to Sa Neo.

But she waited and waited and nothing happened. Instead, she just saw dark emptiness and slowly, fear began to grow inside of her. It was the fear that she was crazy, fear that she had imagined traveling to the magical world. Lily couldn't get comfortable and she felt uneasy in the darkness. She knew she needed to clear her mind in order to tedimeta, the way she would transport to the lands, but it didn't feel right. And so she reluctantly climbed back upstairs.

Why are you scared? she asked herself.

It didn't feel right, she answered back. *I need to make the space my own, and feel confident,* she thought.

She went back to her room and looked at her pouch full of the pieces she had collected. The colored crystal stones were all lined up in a row and they glistened with extra brightness. They wanted to go home, she could feel them tell her.

"Soon my little ones," she told them back.

Talking to objects and things around her became quite normal now after visiting Sa Neo. Even though she couldn't see their energy, she knew it existed. She thought back to the initiation ritual with the witches and Queen Jade. The instructions flowed back into her mind effortlessly as though the ritual had taken place merely moments ago. How she needed to create a sacred space and give gratitude to the elements that ruled the world. Air, nature, water, fire.

Lily cleared her dressing table in her room and sat down to begin preparing her sacred space. The ingredients to complete her vision seemed to call out to her organically. Although they were from this world, she could feel their energy was laid from many worlds before, constantly being reinvented, re-incarnated into something new. She placed the objects around into an even square, creating an imaginary cross.

"Air," Lily said as she lit an incense stick. The smell of burnt resin wafted through the air, creating a beautiful aroma to cleanse the space upon where she stood. Lily spoke words of gratitude to the air as she smudged the aromatic incense around herself, creating a vortex of energy swirling around in abundance.

"I allow the air to clean this sacred space and bring clarity to my mind, open my heart, and bring me forth to you again," she whispered out loud, feel the confidence inside her growing again slowly.

"Fire," Lily chanted, as she lit a small candle, staring at the glowing purr. She loved the way the flame danced before her; it moved unpredictably as she blew softly on it. She wondered if she was tormenting the flame as she teased it lovingly, or whether the flame enjoyed being teased? Lily stared deeply into the flame, feeling the creative energy ignite within herself.

"Water," Lily said as she took a big sip of water, thinking about the way it refreshed her body and mind. The water revitalized her, it cleansed her thoughts, washing away any negative talk or limiting beliefs that she had. She poured the cup of water into a small bowl and watched the way it trickled down as a soft rainfall. If she was present and still enough, she could hear the water sing musical love notes to her like it did in her dream. The water splashed in the bowl and sung their own song of gratitude for having been reunited with each other once again. It was an appraisal of hallelujah as it escaped one side and jumped into the other. For she had created a change, a path to freedom, and a rebellion of the usual routine where it swam within the same circle of waters. Lily placed the bowl down and took a deep breath in.

Mother Nature, she heard the voice inside her say as she lifted a palmful of dirt in her hand that she had collected from the garden. She rubbed the grains of dirt between her fingers as it slowly fell into the bowl of water below. As the dirt molded with the water it created a muddy paste, and she gleefully dove her fingers deep into the bowl, enjoying the change of textures that she had now created.

Although the dirt and water had separated, a murky color of brown stained the surface of the bowl, concealing the magic that was playing within.

"I give thanks to Mother Nature," she said softly as she closed her eyes. "And to the water, thank you for your gift of purity, replenishment, and cleanliness. To air, thank you for my breath. Now to fire, the magical creator of light without which life is not born, thank you for your gift." As Lily finished her speech of gratitude, she could both feel and see a swirling force of energy light up all around her. The swirl of colors and vibrating lights cocooned around her like a tight bubble, all exuding the same emotion—a feeling of peace and nurturing support. Lily sighed with relief as she relaxed deeply into the bubble of light. Her mind cleared effortlessly as she surrendered any thoughts that didn't support her wishes to return to Sa Neo. With confidence and grace she imagined her body become lighter, and as expected, she began to levitate. High above the sky, she traveled. Completely weightless, not thinking about anything, except how immensely full of love and peace she was.

three

The Arrival

As Lily opened her eyes to the red crystal beach of Otor she felt a rush of excitement leap from inside her belly up high into the sky. It was true, she had traveled to Sa Neo again! The red hue of the crystals gleamed brightly from the blazing sun, and Lily was relieved that the energy felt exactly the same way as it did before—a nurturing and calming sensation. She picked up one of the crystal rocks and skidded it across the ocean, watching it fall down deep below. *Indigo,* she thought. No one appeared to be around, but Lily didn't want to make the same mistake as her last visit, so she walked to the far edge of the beach, near the rock pools, where she could hide before calling her mermaid friends. The rock pools felt warm to touch, and the little sea creatures curled into their shells as she walked over them to the edge of the ocean.

Lily kneeled down on a crystal slab that was hidden behind a large rock and pulled out her Ouroboros snake charm necklace. She softly ran her finger over the surface as she relived the memories in her mind. The snake scales etched out on the golden trinket crinkled beneath her skin; it was the opposite texture to the smoothness of the eyes. Each eye was a different color, one black pearl and one white crystal. The two sides of opposite together equaling one, and together they formed the eyes of her beloved necklace. She felt as though the Ouroboros talked to her. She loved how the snake's mouth ate its own tail, the memory of life, never-ending, forever circulating and infinitely spinning. As she stared at the symbol that connected her to them, she thought about how badly she missed her mermaid friends. And she scolded herself for waiting so long to return to the magical world.

Lily dangled the Ouroboros necklace in the water's edge. As soon as the Ouroboros touched the water she felt as though she could hear dying screams shrieking in the far distance, and she shivered. *What was that?* she wondered. She dismissed the noise as just her imagination and closed her eyes to prepare for contact. Lily envisioned a line of communication, telepathically linking her to Indigo. Connecting her to the same merman that she kept seeing in her dreams. Before he was a child, laying in her arms, and now, who was he?

The waves in the ocean began to stir as a strong current fled toward her, as though a streamline pipe had burst below and was shooting water away. She could sense him coming closer. From the water below two eyes appeared. They were dark, black eyes like the Indigo child she remembered; they pierced through her heart and she felt his strength, his connection, his Soul.

"Indigo!" Lily smiled, saying his name loudly as he surfaced from the ocean.

Indigo had grown up quickly. His chest was now defined with strength, and his black hair swept heavily across his face. But it was his eyes that she remembered. So intensely dark and holding wisdom from centuries past, she could feel his heart beating through his gaze. He looked exactly the same from the dreams that she had been having. But when he opened his mouth, his words spoke no pleasure.

"What do you want?" he scowled, his face furious with anger.

"I'm Lily ..."

"I don't care who you are. Why and how did you call me?"

She could feel his hatred beyond his eyes. They weighed heavy with grief from the dark bottom of his heart. A bitter taste of rage laced through his words and Lily had never felt so insignificant in all her life. The visions of her dreams now puzzled her, tormenting her head as though she had played a cruel trick upon herself.

"Crysanthe said we would always be connected," Lily tried again, displaying her necklace to prove her worth.

"Don't speak of the great Crysanthe as though you knew her," Indigo argued back as he threw his head to the side, displaying a small scar on the side of his ear. "I know who you are. You've brought nothing but shame to our community."

His eyes darted back and forth at Lily; he was livid. And Lily could feel his disgust. She felt as though he hated the way she looked, the way she breathed and how she walked. She wasn't of his breed, and for that, he hated her.

"I dreamed that you were in trouble," Lily spoke, almost pleading with her words as she moved closer.

The old Lily would have run away by now, but she was stronger, more able to handle the truth. She felt in her bones that she needed to stand strong. Her presence would apologize for the damage she had done. *We were friends once, why is Sa Neo so different now?* she wondered.

"I'm in trouble?" Indigo laughed, but it was a nervous laugh with hints of aggression. Lily felt confused. "Go and see the blood by your hands at the orange beach," he continued as he pointed behind him.

"But I ..."

"Listen, I don't want you to call me again. We are not connected," Indigo interrupted, looking at her with half-squinted eyes, as though he didn't even want to give her his full attention, deeming her unworthy.

Lily shook her head with disbelief.

"Please, just listen ..." Lily didn't dare take her eyes off him, she couldn't. She felt a strangely profound connection with him. A feeling that she had never experienced before. She wondered if their connection had existed from lifetimes before. "I was there when you were first born," Lily continued; he didn't move, and Lily took it as a sign to keep going. "Your merpeople said I was a blessing to your world, and that I was allowed to gift you a name. It was I who named you Indigo." Lily kept talking, feeling as though her words were soothing like a childhood story. And Indigo for the first time didn't look angry; instead, he listened. No words, no questions, just listened. "This is the reason why we have the same Ouroboros necklace, you see." Lily showed her necklace to Indigo, displaying it proudly. "It's from my world, not yours. It never belonged to the mermaids. That was the greatest mystery of it all." Lily paused as she looked to Indigo, who now floated closer to her. She could feel the anger in his essence was slowly changing, and that he too wanted to understand. Even though he may have been too proud to ask for help in understanding, she could sense a glimmer in his Soul that he wanted to try. The feeling of anger that separated them was evident only on his side, when he believed it, but when Lily changed her thinking to believing that there was love between them, the space around them changed.

Indigo reached forward gently, to which Lily mirrored the same action. And in seconds they were face to face. She could feel the coolness of his skin breathing on her. The depth of his dark-blue eyes, so dark they engulfed all light and her thoughts slipped through them. He lifted his hand slowly toward her, but Lily was too mesmerized by his eyes and she didn't realize what he was doing. In a quick movement he grabbed the piece of jewelry around her throat and pulled on it tightly.

"Give me your necklace!" he shouted through his teeth, the anger once again seeping through his eyes.

But the clasp was sealed tight, and he dragged her down by the neck, smashing her to the ground with a loud smack. Lily screamed. His slimy hands now held a better grip, and he tore the necklace apart in one smooth motion.

"There, the connection is cut." He laughed obnoxiously, showing the Ouroboros necklace in his hand, "Now leave me alone!"

He dove deep below the ocean, creating a small tornado of waves behind him. And as a natural effect up above, the clouds mirrored the same action, spinning around hurriedly and violently spitting out rain, thunder, and lightning.

Lily stood up and rubbed her chin; a small cut had pierced through the skin. She let the blood drip onto her hand, staring at the mark of what had happened. The pain felt numb, like it didn't exist. But the pain of her bruised ego beat overpoweringly loud. A friendship that was once sealed between the two had been broken, and her necklace that she wore proudly around her neck for so many years had gone, just like that. She washed her bleeding chin in the ocean, cupping some water to cleanse the wound. Upon touching the salty water the stinging pain oozed into her reality and the tears started to roll down her cheeks. How was it so? She wasn't a child anymore, and yet the tears flooded from her eyes too quickly. She couldn't hold them in. *Wasn't it meant to get easier as you got older? Why did things seem more confusing than before?* she wondered.

She had been to Sa Neo; she knew this world, and yet somehow it had changed again so drastically. Yet if she was to remember the lessons correctly, the core belief of this world implied that she was the creator, even though everything felt as though it was being created against her. *Why am I creating this?* After days of seeing the signs but not listening, she had taken a leap of faith to travel and see her friends. She thought this was what her Soul had been crying for. What her heart had been asking her for. And she listened to herself, saying that this would be the adventure that she had been seeking, that it was the missing puzzle. But she listened to her heart and now look where it led her. Alone, worried, and lost. The old feeling that she held when she first visited Sa Neo was nowhere to be found anymore. It had completely disappeared. And it had traveled so far away that she couldn't even remember how it was the way she felt as a small girl. All she knew was that something wasn't right.

Lily dusted the stony rubble off her knees. The rain from the clouds above continued to pour heavily. She had never felt that kind of storm before and she knew she needed to get shelter quickly. She closed her eyes and took a deep breath, telling herself that it was time to start over. And with those words she took off deep into the wild forest, along the path toward Karisma's house.

four

Tattoo Faces

The laneway to Karisma's was nothing like Lily remembered it to be. It was full of broken pebbles that were carved down to a fine round texture, as though someone had walked over them a million times. As Lily walked along the path she had visions of the crystal bricks when they had first been laid. She could see the person who placed each and every brick on that path, and how they poured their thoughts and energetic vibrations into the pavement. Every crystal brick that touched the ground and absorbed the dirt for one to walk on seemed to exude great emotions and Lily felt like she knew the person very well. She wondered how it was that she could see such visions and feel their strength underneath her feet.

Lily followed the pathway to Karisma's front door, which from what she remembered used to be painted red. But now, the edges of the wood withered with age, torn down by the rain and thunder, and a great big lock hung on the outside, one that needed a giant key to open. But the lock was broken and she couldn't remember there being a lock on the door either.

"Psst," came a noise from Lily's left, but when she looked, nothing was there.

"Come closer," she heard it whisper again, and a faint outline of a shadow wavered lightly.

"I can't see you," Lily said as the ball of clouded smoke came closer to her. "Karisma, is that you?" Lily asked, wondering why Karisma would be hiding from her.

"Be careful, the moons are fullest tonight," the voice said again, as it blew stronger toward Lily, pushing her toward the front of Karisma's house.

That's odd. Lily thought as she watched the colored smoke float up high above the treetops. Lily knew that when the moons were full, it meant that a witches' ceremony was taking place, but it would usually be a joyous celebration, not one to be feared. Lily continued along the path but when she walked through the door, it appeared to be completely abandoned, with Karisma nowhere to be found. The ceramic cups that hung on the walls in the kitchen were broken, and the beautiful living area where Lily once lay her head upon silk pillows were torn down. Instead, Karisma's tree-trunk home was wildly overgrown with plants and leaves, full of insects and lizards. The plants grew in thick canopies around the house, spinning the room as though it were its own web, and in the corner sat the most peculiar creature. The body was that of a beautiful young girl. She had long flowing pink hair with green streaks through it. But her face was covered in a thick black tattoo. The tattoo was decorated with many dots that wove around in circles with long lines from the tip of her head down to her neck.

"Hello, my name is Lily," Lily said as she waved to the odd-looking girl.

"Eb aefs." the girl tried to reply, and she tilted her face from side to side, coughing the words through her small mouth.

It was here that Lily could see she was being held by something, for she tried to raise her arms, but they appeared stuck together, and she wasn't just sitting in the corner, she was unable to move completely.

"Is that you, Karisma?" Lily asked, wondering if perhaps she had been held beneath some kind of spell, for she never had that color hair before. Although Lily knew that Karisma was far too powerful for something like that to happen.

The tattoo faced girl blinked her eyes quickly and then looked toward the door where a long corridor stretched out. Lily remembered that tunnel well. Each of the giant roots from the tree connected to the other lands, and it was a way to explore the world without tedimetaing. Lily moved closer to the tattooed girl, and when she looked into her eyes, she could tell that it wasn't Karisma.

"Help me," the girl said, but the words didn't come out of her mouth. Instead, Lily felt as though the creature spoke telepathically to her. Or was it Lily's own intuition she was hearing? The voices from her heart spoke loudly in Sa Neo, for this was the place where she learned how to listen to her intuition. And it was a lesson that she continued to practice even after her travels here. She thought back to before she found this world, and how she used to ignore the voice in her heart; what a foolish little girl she once was. The old Lily would get too caught up in her own head, too worried about what other people thought, and seldom allowed her own ideas to shine. But, now here she was, walking into the same land with a new set of eyes, and seeing everything completely differently. Because it wasn't the same land anymore. It had changed just as much as she had; years had passed and like she, the land had grown into something new. So Lily did all she could do: embrace the change, and become curious as to what kind of world this place was going to be. Despite how eerie and creepy it appeared.

"I'll go look down here," Lily explained to the girl, waving as she turned to signal her departure.

The tattoo-faced girl half smiled. But it was a cold expression; if Lily wasn't feeling so optimistic, the old version of herself would have feared such a strange response and read into it as though it were a double meaning. She would have questioned its motives, and why it was smiling that way to her, and whether she was walking into danger. But now, she knew there was no danger. She would be fine. She knew that she held the power over her thoughts in her head, and that she had love for herself. That was the greatest weapon that one could use.

Lily walked along the corridor into the first room on the right. She wasn't sure what had pulled her toward this room, nor why she should go in there. But when she opened the door, she felt as though all became apparent. The room was full of ancient books piled on top of each other from the floor to the ceiling. And even spread across the ceiling were books opened with beautiful imagery and words. She felt safe just being in the presence of such a space for the weight of the words around her felt magnetically enchanting. It was as though each individual person who wrote their heart and Soul into those pages were still living and breathing right next to her. A large open window allowed light to fill the room naturally and from the outside, a branch from a tree had swept in, bending to the floor, creating a perfectly flat table for someone to use. But there was no chair in front of the table; instead, there was a plain wooden box, a small bowl, a red candle, a small jar, and a feather. A soft breeze moved through the window. It filtered through her curly hair and grazed gently against her skin. The breeze tickled all her senses at once, sending a quick shiver over her body. And with a strong force of energy, she walked over to the shelf on the far right, and picked out a book.

Spells to Reveal Your Authentic Self, it read.

Lily opened the book to the middle as the smell of stale pages wafted through the air. A puff of smoke rose from the book, and in front of Lily hovered a very old, very wrinkly woman.

"Welcome to the Spell for Transformation," she said, looking Lily directly in the eyes.

The old lady had clear, glass marble eyes and her eyelids sagged over the edges of them heavily. *She has been around for many lives, and must hold many stories,* Lily thought as she stared at the mystical old woman. A bright printed scarf was wrapped around the lady's head, holding what little hair she had in place. Around her neck was the strangest sight, for she wore eight gold circle necklaces that reached right up to beneath her chin and at the base of the necklace flowed a red silk top which matched the printed scarf around her head precisely.

"Are you ready?" The old lady lowered her eyes to focus on Lily as she glared with a tinge of impatience.

"Yes, yes," Lily replied, with her best manners. "I'm looking for a spell to release someone, is this correct?"

"You don't ask for the spell, you open the book and the spell comes to you," the old lady replied, although she didn't look at Lily. "Okay, let's get started. First, the bowl." The old lady pointed to the bowl on the wooden table, which levitated slightly.

Lily picked it up and placed it in front of her.

"For this spell, you will need fennel, black pepper, cinnamon oil, the petals of a sweet pea flower, and a stalk of ivy," the old lady said as she recited the spell from the memory of her mind.

"How am I to find all of that?" Lily asked, frowning sadly.

"The box of crosses," the lady replied, as she pointed to the box, which was now carved out with geometric shapes on it.

Lily leaned over the table and picked up the box. As she opened the lid an assortment of herbs, spices, and flowers protruded. The aroma of the flora and fauna stirred around the room, and the old witch lady smiled, sensing the beginning of magic commencing.

"Good. Very good," the old lady said as she opened her mouth wide and smiled, almost laughing, displaying soft pink gums with no teeth. "Now, pick up each piece, crush it in your hands, and place it in the bowl," she instructed as all the ingredients in the wooden box lifted up and patiently waited their turn.

Lily did as she was told, putting each ingredient into the bowl. She enjoyed touching the different textures as she crumbled the leaves and flowers with her bare hands. The scent of each item stained her skin. But Lily felt as though it was with pleasure. For she believed that perhaps the item wanted to share its blessing to all who touched it, and by sharing that scent of bliss, she in return would think of the plant, bringing it to life once more. As each item fell into the bowl below it started to swirl, mixing itself together.

"Rae di wa sa lee. Ill a peh tag me noir," the old lady chanted above, bringing the spell to life. "Read the words below, dear," she said as she pointed at the book.

Each word lifted up off the page as she recited it, embedding the spell with her own support, her own dedication.

"With this spell I transition from one to another. I transform into my Higher Self, my ultimate light."

As Lily said the words out loud, the air blew strongly through the tree and into the room, swirling around Lily and the old lady. The old lady closed her eyes lightly as she continued to chant softly. At last, one great big gust of wind pushed through the bowl, lifting the mixture high into the air and compressing the potion into a small jar.

"It's ready," the old lady said as she opened her eyes. But the marble clarity in her eyes was no longer visible; a dark red had taken over. As though the spell had transformed her.

"And what do I do?" Lily asked, as she peered over the small jar that was now packed tightly.

"Pick a leaf from the tree. Take the feather here and dip it into the jar; it will turn to ink."

Lily pulled a large leaf from the tree that hung outside the window. With the small feather she touched the tip into the jar which then dripped with a thick ink as described.

"Now write 'Transformation' in big letters on the leaf. Go on."

Lily wasn't sure if she even knew how to spell the word, although surely she did. Perhaps it was just the pressure of someone else around her. But it didn't matter, for when she put the feather to the leaf it began to take on a mind of its own. Writing in the most beautiful calligraphy-style writing that definitely was not Lily's handwriting.

"Burn the leaf over the fire from the candle and set your intention. Think about what it is that you wish to achieve by doing this."

The flame of the red candle illuminated when the word "fire" was spoken and Lily lifted the leaf to hover it above the fire. As she did so she thought about the word transformation and what it actually meant. Even though this spell was for the trapped girl, Lily somehow applied the lesson to herself. The idea of becoming the greatest version of herself was surely something that she also wished to attain. Although she now knew the steps needed to really love herself, she still felt as though there was something inside of her that was lacking. A voice that held guilt from the past, perhaps? Or was it fear of who she really was? Here, this land told her she held great wisdom. And yet, when she returned to her own world, she felt as though her wisdom was something that everyone had on some level or another. *How can I feel the strength and knowledge of my own abilities in the real world?* she wondered.

The leaf burned slowly above the flame, and as the smoke rose high above, it seeped through the house, covering the ceiling in a thick blanket. It moved through the hallways and into the room where the spider-girl was. Lily felt a longing to follow it, but she wanted to ensure the spell had been complete.

As though the old lady felt her thoughts, she whispered, "And so it is." Then she disappeared, along with the book. All that was left was a tiny jar filled with dusty smoke, and Lily was standing all alone in a room, full of old, dusty books.

Lily took the jar and put it into her pouch, then walked back to the lounge area where the tattoo-faced girl once was. But alas, she too was here no longer. And in front of Lily stood a beautiful child wearing a short green dress. She was no older than eight or nine years old and she reminded Lily of herself when she was younger. The tattoo on the girl's face had disappeared, and she giggled with a great smile.

"You're going to save us," the young girl whispered to Lily as she ran past her and back along the corridor.

Lily ran behind her, following the green dress.

"Who are you?" Lily asked as she ran up to the small child.

The girl said nothing more, and with her left hand, she pointed to the corridor on the right.

"This is where we need you." And with her right hand, she pulled out a green citrine crystal, closed her eyes, and disappeared.

Lily looked to the corridor that the child had pointed to. It was very dark, and it felt cold to touch. The floor was covered in dirt, and the walls were lined with mushy moss as well as strange flowers that grew in dark places. But despite the darkness, the walkway was lit up by small fire beetles that buzzed above her head. And Lily thought how lucky there was to be darkness for these fire beetles to be able to shine so brightly. The beetles flew by quickly, sparking a beam of light that appeared and disappeared as quickly as a shooting star. They all flew deeper into the cave, as though signaling the path upon which Lily was to follow. Lily peered to the edge of the cave. It was cold and dark. She wasn't even sure where it would take her, or what lay beneath. All she knew was that her friends were nowhere, the mermaids hated her, and she came back for a reason. Despite facing the unknown, she had no other options. She couldn't live with the idea of what if ... she couldn't turn back now. And so, like the fireflies that flew above her, a flame ignited within her own heart, lighting her Soul with strength and courage, and with a twinkling of excitement shooting through her body, she took a deep breath, and entered the tunnel.

five

Praza, the 2nd Land

The tunnel beneath the lands challenged Lily greatly. She had walked for so long that she felt weary from exhaustion. Her feet hurt, and the damp air that surrounded her was now cushioning her breath, her chest, and her ability to breathe or think clearly. If she did think about it, anxious feelings would creep in. It would overtake her mind, her thoughts and her sanity. If she looked at herself in one light, she was stuck beneath a giant tree, walking through the veins of its roots. Roots that magically connected lands and villages. She had no idea how far away the next village was, nor whether it would be open to receiving her, nor if anyone would be there at all! Where were all her friends? She felt completely alone. As Lily walked, she reminded herself of why she had traveled to Sa Neo in the first place. She was following her dream, and it never said anything about being easy. But still, she had to listen; if not, they would haunt her. She could still hear Indigo's plea for help so vividly in her head and she could see his eyes, the black empty pools that stained her heart and pierced a hole into it deeply. There was an undeniable flame that ignited between them, unable to be extinguished. The feeling of needing to help him despite his hatred for her overtook her logical thinking.

Even though she felt completely naked without her Ouroboros necklace, her connection to the mermaid world, she knew it wouldn't be forever and that something wonderful would change and turn around in its place. She tried to soothe her fears with positive thinking. She had two ways to look at it: one, she was walking through the cold tunnel deep beneath the lands, unsure where she was going, or where she would end up; or two, she could think about all the wonderful things that may lay on the other side, she could change her mind to hopeful thoughts. Perhaps there would be sunshine, glowing rainbows, and a warm cup of hot chocolate waiting for her. As Lily continued to walk through the tunnel, she imagined the feeling of that delicious sweet cacao as it drizzled down her throat and flooded warmth to her whole body. The cold tunnel suddenly didn't feel so cold anymore. Instead, the fireflies began to buzz around her again like fireworks, creating patterns of vibrant electricity. They looked like small stars and flowers, bursting from the core as they exploded in fast motion. Lily smiled, a mischievous smile, remembering how wonderful and magical this world around her truly was. Her excitement to see the end of the tunnel sparked motivation inside of her, and she walked briskly, feeling a burst of energy shoot through her body, identical to the dance of the fireflies.

After several more minutes the tunnel began to glow lighter, and before Lily knew it, she had arrived. But before Lily exited, she peeked her head out of the tree trunk to see if anyone was near; there was no one besides a few small monkeys that hung in the branches. As Lily walked up the land, she noticed that the air felt slightly cooler than the land of Otor; it had more moisture for it smelled like it had rained often, and there were many water channels moving around where Lily stood. Lily looked beneath her feet to see what color crystal lay before her. It was the color orange. A soft, milky-colored orange. She placed it in her pocket.

The sky was a mixture of smoke and soft orange hues, and Lily could see large volcanoes bursting in the far distance. They exploded in the sky like a rocket, creating a mass destruction in the atmosphere and blowing up everything in sight. The beach could be seen in the far distance to her right, but there was no one around, just a few pathways that weaved through the shallow lakes and over little bridges. Lily took the first path that she was standing on. It was long and windy and took her further into the forest. She walked across bridges and between high mountains until the pathway finally stopped in front of a small shabby house with two levels, made out of bamboo. The roof was covered with large palm tree leaves and on the side of the house colorful sheets were draped over branches that blew gently in the wind from side to side. The sheets were orange with white mandala patterns that started in the center and moved outwards, creating a beautiful big flower. On the front of the door was another sign saying "Marlina Residence." Lily knocked on the door.

A little girl, no older than five, answered it. She didn't say anything. She just looked at Lily while holding a toy doll in her hand. The young girl wore two pigtails high in her hair with orange bows tied around them. Her doll was ragged with torn clothes; it looked like it had been handed down for many generations.

"Hello, my name is Lily and ..." but before Lily could finish her sentence, the young girl had opened the door wide, signaling for Lily to come through.

"I know who you are," the little girl whispered, and she began to skip down the hallway, encouraging Lily to follow her. "She's here!" she yelled out.

"Come through," an older woman said as she poked her head from the end of the hallway and waved to Lily, smiling eagerly.

Lily walked down the corridor and followed the little girl until she reached a kitchen where two other children were sitting, a boy and a girl. The girl who answered the door holding her doll had sat down in between the other children. A delicious display of tea and muffins lay proudly on the table and the children sat quietly, waiting patiently.

"It's so lovely to meet you, Lily!" The older lady smiled as she spoke, and came forward to hug Lily tightly with a small squeeze on her shoulders, perhaps a little too hard though. "My name is

Marlina," she continued, nodding with empathy. She had a peculiar stare in her eyes; it hovered over Lily's stance, but in a loving way. It was as though her eyes could see everything that had ever happened in Lily's life, and strangely, it comforted Lily to be able to share her own story. Marlina's hair was perfectly kept, parted in the middle, cut short above her shoulders. She wore an apron painted with orange stripes and white diamonds. And beneath it was an A-line dress, perfectly ironed, made from matching colored cotton.

"These are my children," she continued, presenting each child with great admiration. "Airlie, whom you've met. Leafy, my boy, he is eight, and Oceana is my eldest." As each name was recited, the child stood up, nodded with a smile and sat back down; however, it was all too perfectly synchronized and Lily felt quite uneasy. She knew children liked to misbehave; but never had she seen such obedient children in all her life.

"It's lovely to meet you all, thank you for welcoming me so unexpectedly into your home," Lily replied, standing awkwardly, unsure what to do.

"It wasn't unexpectedly," blurted Airlie, fiddling with the hair of her doll.

"It wasn't?" Lily asked, searching their faces for answers.

"Of course not." Marlina smiled, lifting a chair for Lily to sit down on. "We knew you were coming. We made this in honor of you. This tea is our local specialty, and ginger biscuits are your favorite, right?" Marlina continued as she poured some tea into an orange triangular cup with small purple lines and handed Lily some biscuits on a matching plate. The aroma of the tea smelt like peppermint, and it dripped through the air, opening the space with clarity.

"How did you know I was coming?" Lily asked, surprised, looking at the three children who were all presented so perfectly, as though preparing themselves all morning for a visit, and yet Lily only knew herself that she would visit Sa Neo not long ago.

"Oceana dreamed that today would be the day," Marlina said as she pointed to the oldest girl who stood up again as her name was recited, curtseying politely. She appeared to be no more than ten years old with chubby cheeks. Her hair was brushed back and fastened with a small butterfly clip on the side. She wore an orange cotton dress, with small bell sleeves and white shoes. Her eyes were incredibly unusual, for around the pupils were drawn-out black circles, as though the pupil continued in the eye, but with a shadow around them.

"I knew you would come, I just knew it!" Oceana said with a great emphasis of bursting energy.

"And you know who I am?" Lily asked as she sipped on the delicious peppermint tea. Upon doing so she felt the airways in her body completely open up, clearing her throat, nose, and mind.

"You are here to save us," whispered a voice in Lily's ear, but no one's lips moved.

"You are the girl who set the tattoo-faced lady free," Marlina replied, smiling with great admiration for Lily.

"In Otor? But that only just happened. Didn't it?" Lily asked, perplexed as to how the news of her actions had traveled so fast.

"Did it?" The mother winked.

"I thought so." Lily recalled her visit thoroughly in her head, wondering if she had remembered it correctly. "How did you know?"

"Your ancestors told us. Did it not happen?" Marlina asked, although she smiled when asking, knowing the truth that it did.

"We all saw it." Airlie giggled, holding her doll to her face. The doll now looked brand new, wearing a checkered dress and an orange ribbon in her hair. Lily was sure that it didn't look that perfect before.

"Shh, Airlie!" Marlina said as she hushed the little girl. "It's okay, Lily, things will feel a little strange as you get readjusted, you've been gone a long time."

Lily nodded in agreement. It was true; she hadn't visited Sa Neo in many years. Yet, she had never met Marlina and her family, nor visited the land of Praza where she now stood. *How was it that they knew so much?* Lily wondered. But despite the safety that Lily felt in the house, she wasn't ready to ask such questions, nervous that they knew the truth about what had happened the last time she visited. The thoughts tormented Lily as it was, and to have to talk about them with complete strangers worried Lily more than she could handle. So instead, she ignored her questions and took a bite of a ginger biscuit.

"Oh, these are delicious!" Lily exclaimed as the biscuit crumbled delicately in her mouth, and hints of roasted caramel oozed over her tongue.

"Leafy here made them," Marlina said as she pointed to her son who looked down shyly.

"They truly are marvelous, thank you!" Lily encouraged, prompting a smile from Leafy. And as he did so, his ears wiggled, pushing the hair away from his face and displaying pointed pixie ears. Marlina fixed Leafy's hair to cover the ears back up, and she winked at Lily again while doing so.

"I love cooking. Here, try this one," Leafy said as he handed another one to Lily.

"Unbelievable!" Lily replied as she took a bite. It tasted completely different, orange and lime scents with cinnamon swirls. "I would love to learn how to make these."

"We can teach you anything." Marlina said. "But first, we need to prepare. The three moons are the fullest tonight."

It was the same words that the shadow said near Karisma's house, and Lily wondered if the two were connected.

"Should we take Lily to the fisherman's edge?" Airlie asked, and as she did so, two beautiful white wings started to open up behind her shoulders.

"Yes, Airlie," Marlina replied as she patted the edges of the wings proudly. "But would you take Lily to the village to collect some water first please? It's good to have some strong arms around here."

"I'm scared of the water," Oceana confessed to Lily, realizing that it looked like she should be the one who was to carry the water for the family, being the oldest, but she just couldn't do it.

"It's okay, Oceana," Marlina soothed, raising her eyebrows lightly and nodding. "Come now, dears," she continued, as she escorted the children and Lily to the front door.

Lily set off with the three children into the village. Airlie and Leafy each held a hand of Lily's, and Oceana walked up ahead, creating a protective triangle.

The village was a series of huts that lined up along a long orange crystal-pebbled street. In the center of the village was a giant circle fountain with a statue in the middle. The statue was breathtaking. It was a woman playing a flute with two long plaits in her hair. The water overflowed from beneath the seat where the woman sat, as though the sound of her playing the flute prompted the water to expel. As Lily walked closer, she could hear the sound of the flute singing above the splashes of water. There were five other people fetching water from the well. A tall lady held a large pot, and she filled up the water through a long tube. It looked far too big and heavy to be able to be taken anywhere, and a little butterfly sat on the lady's shoulder with bright orange wings that circled around her back.

"Is this ..." the tall lady stood up and asked, walking closer to Lily.

As she walked closer, Lily could see that she had the same tattooed face as the spider girl in Karisma's tree house.

"Yes," Oceana replied confidently. "It is She."

The tall lady bowed in a low bend, and she smiled, looking Lily in the eyes. "You take care now," she laughed as she finished tipping the water through the tube. She then touched the outer edge of the large pot and as she did so, the pot shrunk to the size of a tiny pebble. Placing the pebble into her pocket, the tattoo-faced lady left the fountain, with the butterfly following her quickly.

"How does she know who I am?" Lily asked as she looked at the children; they were all smiling eerily at her—a weird, uncanny knowingness of everything—and yet Lily had no idea what was happening herself.

"We've been waiting a long time for you," Airlie replied with her orange cupid's bow lips.

"Although we all have conflicting reasons for why you're here," Leafy muttered under his breath as he rolled his eyes.

Lily nodded awkwardly, pretending she understood what Leafy had said, and she looked at the townsfolk trying to gauge some information. She was surrounded with various witches, fairies, gnomes, dwarfs, pixies, every enchanting creature she could imagine. They all appeared to be doing their own thing, but every now and again Lily would catch them staring at her and she felt uneasy.

"Don't worry about them, you're safe while you are with us three," Leafy said as he handed Lily a bucket and together they drew water from the beautiful fountain. The sound of the flute on the statue lady grew louder, and Airlie began to sing a sweet melody as she thanked the woman for the gift of water.

A loud smash of thunder broke the harmonious sound in the air and everyone around the village looked up to the sky, now seeing a thick blanket of dark-orange clouds covering the sun. Sparks of lightning sliced through the clouds, and a chaotic sound of thunder followed after shortly. The village folk all ran for cover, and Lily looked to the children, terrified.

"Is it?" Airlie looked to Oceana who nodded stiffly, and she began to run back to the house.

"Come quickly," Leafy said as he ran after Oceana.

Lily and Airlie held hands as they ran away from the town, neither one looking back.

"What's happening?" Lily asked as they arrived back home, holding the buckets of water that splashed to the ground from running so quickly.

"The moons are fullest tonight," Oceana said, but the words that came out of her mouth held no emotion. It was as though she didn't say them.

"Oh, I'm so happy you are back safely," Marlina said as she closed the windows and doors tightly. "Come, let's fill the bath up."

The children all followed Marlina holding buckets of water, except for Oceana. And one by one they walked upstairs to pour the water into a giant bathtub.

"Thank you so much, Lily, you've been a great help," Marlina said as the bathtub filled up with water.

"Perhaps, Leafy and Airlie, you could show Lily how we get the blood from the frankincense tree? We'll need it for tonight's ceremony."

"Okay," Leafy replied, directing Lily and Airlie outside.

"Oceana, can you stay here? I need your help," Marlina instructed, as the two stood in the bathroom, waving the children goodbye.

Lily followed Airlie and Leafy behind the house to a wonderfully tall tree. Leafy walked up to the trunk, put his hand on it and whispered. As soon as he did so the sap from the tree bled fiercely beneath his hand and it pushed out in rhythmic heartbeats like pulsating liquid. Leafy took out a small wooden box and held it beneath the wood, capturing the sap into the box until it overflowed. Once in the wooden box the sap hardened in small circles.

"It's frankincense, do you know it?" Leafy asked as he walked over to another great big tree, folding the small box up into a tiny pebble and putting it in his pocket, the same way the tattoo-faced lady had done with her bucket at the fountain.

Lily shook her head.

"It smells sweet," Airlie said as she smiled and played with her doll, which had changed back into the raggedy, torn clothes beneath the sunlight.

"We'll use this to cleanse ourselves after it's done," Leafy added in as he looked to Airlie, who was now holding her doll tightly and smiling to herself.

"After what's done?" Lily asked as she moved to the tree to smell the leaves. Airlie was right, the scent of the trees was sweet, almost with light spices. And Lily felt lighter standing near it, breathing it in.

"After the ceremony's done," Leafy replied, collecting the sap from the last tree and guiding them back toward the house. "It will protect us. Here, keep this safe. Don't tell anyone you have it."

Leafy handed Lily a small pebble full of the frankincense which she put into her pouch. Although by now, Lily was feeling most uneasy as she recalled the ceremony from her last visit to Sa Neo and she subtly reached into her bag to pull out her amethyst ring. The ring fastened effortlessly on her finger, and she felt stronger in herself just from wearing it. Memories of the lessons she learned from Karisma and Violetta flashed through her mind, and she predicted her escape route in case the time came. She remembered the spell of invisibility, or she could always tedimeta to another land.

Lily and the two children walked back to the house. Marlina was in the kitchen sitting with a paper and pen. She was writing something down.

"Oh, how wonderful for your return, welcome back," Marlina said as she stood and greeted them.

"We have the resin," Leafy replied as he pulled out six small pebbles and put them onto the table.

Marlina rubbed her hands over the top of the pebbles and as she did so, they reformed back into their original shape, overflowing with the tree's blood. Leafy pulled out two silver trays and sat them on the bench closest to the window beneath the direct sunlight.

"May I ask you all something?" Lily asked as Marlina and Leafy poured the resin onto the silver trays.

"Of course," Marlina replied as she stopped what she was doing to give Lily her full attention.

"Who are the tattoo-faced creatures?" Lily asked, as Leafy and Airlie also stopped what they were doing and looked to Marlina, waiting for her answer. Marlina's face turned grave, and she straightened her neck slightly, blinking several times.

"I'm back," Oceana announced as she interrupted the conversation.

She had changed into a long orange dress with ties on the shoulders; it ballooned out below and stopped just short of her bare feet. Her hair was swept back tightly, plaited and wet. Lily was surprised; she thought she was scared of water.

"Lily was just asking about the tattoo-faced people," Marlina explained as Oceana's face resembled that of her mother's.

The three children all moved closer together and sat at the table, as though they were schoolchildren, waiting for their teacher to fill them in on the information. Lily too took a seat at the table, wondering the truth.

"Well," Marlina began, but there were tears that had surfaced in her eyes, "there are some people in life who were born knowing the strength of their own power. Most of us spend our lives removing the layers of conditioning to get to the truth. But these people knew it from the moment they took their first breath. They walk courageously without fear, knowing their purpose, their right to stand in the world and the necessity of their life in order for evolution, in order for others to come after."

"But that sounds like a wonderful trait, why do I feel like they are sad and hiding?"

"Because ..." Marlina said, nodding to Lily as though she was connecting with her. And she waved her hand over the children's head. "I don't want to upset the children," Marlina whispered. "You see, Allura is our ruler on this land, and when she learned of such gifts, she felt threatened. The leaders don't want us to know how powerful we are. They want to keep us small. And so, those who know the truth are branded, and made to feel uneasy. That branding isn't a tattoo, it's a magical curse, that shields them from being themselves, stops them from fulfilling their destiny."

"Why doesn't anyone rise against Allura?" Lily asked, now irritated knowing the truth of the village's suppression.

"We have never dared speak about it. But we think we know how to get our power," Marlina said, although her voice lowered to a very quiet tone, and the children looked away, out the window as though not listening. "There's an army of pure souls on the land of Naja. They are called the Najatinis. They are the Third Eye of the world," Marlina said, nodding at Lily.

"And these Najatinis will help us, do you think?"

"Well, we can try, right? We need to take back what's owed to us," Marlina said, her voice rising back up now, and she clicked her fingers. "Airlie, hand me a wet rag, please, dear."

The children all looked to one another nervously. Lily felt shaken too, the story was too ghastly, and especially Lily had been faced with such tragedy.

"Airlie, please?" Marlina asked again, but Airlie was still looking away and instead, Leafy stood up and rinsed a washer with some water.

"I trust you, Lily," Marlina said as she gently wiped the edges of her own face. Slowly, a layer of thick cream was removed, and to Lily's surprise, the etching of a deep-seated black tattoo appeared.

"It happened when I was a child. No one else can know, or my children will be in danger. I used to fly through the sky on the back of a dragon. It had thick bold wings, and a belly full of fire. We were no harm to anyone, I only longed to play with others."

The children all squirmed uneasily as they looked to their mother and Lily realized that the children were too all living in fear of being found out.

"That's terrible," Lily said as she looked down to the ground, unsure of where to gaze up to.

She felt so sad for the children having to live in a world where they couldn't be who they wanted to be. Where they weren't free to express themselves in their desired manner. And she wondered about her own world back home, if she was living in alignment with her own authentic truth. And if everyone around her was doing the same.

"There's more," Marlina said, as she stood up. "Children, I think that it's time to show Lily the truth."

six

Fishing

You must hurry before it gets too dark," Marlina said as she waved Lily and the three children goodbye.

Leafy took charge first, leading the pack in an authoritative manner. Lily and Oceana walked directly behind him, and above the three flew Airlie, her wings soaring through the sky.

"She never gets to fly," Oceana said as she smiled while looking up at her younger sister.

The wings on Airlie's shoulders stretched out wide and with each flap inwards they changed color. Every color of the rainbow moved through the little girl, and as she fluttered her wings, tiny droplets of dust danced to the ground. It was beautiful to watch, like snow falling. And as she looked up at Airlie flying, she wondered what it would be like to go through life hiding who you really were. And yet at the same time, Lily couldn't help but feel that perhaps she already knew what that feeling was like, that instead, she was the one who voluntarily hid who she really was, scared to be judged, or misjudged. It was only herself that stopped the real her standing strong in her own light.

"Airlie quickly come down!" Leafy yelled to Airlie who was now far ahead. His ears were pointing toward the trees, and he stopped the children, running to the closest tree and hugging it, pressing his ear tightly against it.

Lily watched with amazement as the lines of the tree trunk move in electrical beats. They amplified like a vibrating drum, sizzling down the line from the branch to the ground.

"There is someone coming! Quick! We need to hide," Leafy said as he ushered the children deeper into the woods.

Airlie landed on the ground and took Leafy's hand while Oceana tucked Airlie's wings into her dress. Leafy walked them to a large tree, where they could hide behind the giant trunk. The small boy kept his ear to the tree, listening to when the path was clear.

Lily felt herself get nervous. It was a strange feeling, being surrounded with locals who lived there and yet they, themselves, were in fear for their own safety. And she felt sad even more, wondering if it was because of her actions that she was the real reason they felt unsafe. Did she do something that changed the fate of their whole world? *I will never forgive myself,* Lily thought as she looked to the children's faces. Their innocence shone brightly behind a protected exterior. Although they seemed happy, Lily wondered how. But perhaps they never knew any different, she told herself.

The sound of galloping horses could be heard from afar, moving closer toward Lily and the children.

"They must be on their way there now," Oceana said as she peeked her eyes above the edge of the tree trunk, as the sound of the horses moved past the children.

"They've gone." Leafy signaled, moving away from the tree, and patted the edges of the roots, thanking the tree for its time.

"Is it safe to walk the path?" Lily asked, worried as she watched Oceana continue to look behind her shoulder.

But the children were strong in courage, and they didn't show any fear, still smiling at Lily.

"We'll walk through the woods but near the path, it's not too much further," Leafy suggested as they crossed over the orange crystal road and deep into the forest on the opposite side.

Here, the trees grew taller, and the ground was covered in tiny orange flowers. Small bees flew from flower to flower, drinking the sweet nectar. Autumn leaves had dropped to the floor, creating a walkway of aged leaves to walk upon. Airlie didn't bring her wings back out, and Lily wondered if she felt confined.

Lily imagined the claustrophobic feeling of wanting to live true to oneself, and yet the restriction of being held back. And perhaps Airlie would never find out just how magical she could be. She was compressed by those who feared someone different, and they just wanted Airlie to conform, terrified of how magnificent she truly could be. Leafy was able to use his gift, and Airlie was able to every now and again, it seemed. But there was an irreplaceable sadness in Oceana. There was something missing in her life. And Lily wondered if, in fact, she didn't have a supernatural gift at all.

The four continued to walk through the forest. Small monkeys ate mangoes up in the treetops, and the sound of crickets laughing could be heard on the trunks nearby. The children giggled with such pleasure of hearing the animals. Little bunny rabbits with orange fur and white spots hopped over the ground as the children walked, and beautiful large butterflies flew above them, as though protecting and guiding them. Airlie looked to their wings, and she smiled as though reliving the feeling of what it felt like to fly.

The four reached the edge of the forest a short time after. And they hid once again, this time behind an orange crystal rock, watching the three horses and the three men who rode them. They appeared to be fishermen.

The three fishermen stood at the point of the beach where a wooden boat was broken in half and cast up ashore. The edges of the boat were covered in slimy moss and had small barnacles attached to the outside; from afar they looked like a small dotted pattern.

"Everyone, stay quiet," Oceana instructed as she took Airlie's hand and moved closer to Lily.

Leafy moved closer to Lily too, and the four huddled together as they peeked carefully around the large crystal rock. Lily felt an immediate urge to protect the children, being the oldest, but at the same time she felt their power was untouched and contained great ability, more than they themselves realized.

The men had tied the horses up to a small tree nearby, and behind one of the horses was a box that was being pulled by a cart. Each of the men wore a hat with a feather in it, and on their face was a tattoo design, similar to the one Lily had seen on the spider girl. One of the men, who wore an orange peacock feather on his hat, moved closest to the shore, and he motioned to the others to follow. The voices were muffled, and the children couldn't hear. It didn't matter, they could see what was happening. And the four watched in silence as a nightmare played out before their eyes.

A beautiful mermaid was being pulled out of the water. It was a very young mergirl who had a brilliant, glowing orange-and-green tail. Her hair was almost as long as her body, and it wrapped around her, tightly like the net around her body. She was caught, and she was terrified. Her fingers clawed through the net in disarray and she watched with screaming eyes as the men pulled her out of the water to her deathly fate. The men snorted with smirks as they dragged the mermaid's body onto sharp rocks. The young mergirl continued to scream, a deafening cry for help as the men handled her roughly. And tears flooded from her eyes, dropping to the stones below in silver droplets, creating a blood-ink stain on the shore where she lay. The men unraveled the net, laughing while doing so. They were used to it. Hunting appeared to be a regular occurrence for them, and they patted each other on the back as though it were a job well done.

Airlie stopped watching, and she nuzzled closely into Oceana, who had also buried her face. It was only Leafy and Lily witnessing the terrible sight.

The men carried the mermaid's body into the wooden casket that was attached with wheels behind the horses. Between the horses and the men, it was the horses who appeared to feel the pain of the mergirl, and they leaped in the air in an attempt to break free, hating their position of being involved in such an act. The men continued to work together and lifted the body into the crate, and once that was finished, they cast the net back out to sea, fastened the horses' reins and jumped back on their backs. They wiped their hands on the clothes they wore, dirtying their outer shell with the same hideous nature that lay within their Souls. And within seconds they had taken off, heading back to the village.

"We must destroy that net!" Lily said as she felt warrior blood shoot through her veins.

"It's magic," Oceana sighed. "We don't have the power to break it."

The rings around Oceana's pupils now swirled around in a different direction and Lily could feel her pain, of wanting to do something but being unable to do so. It was a catastrophe. A desperate plea for change and yet, an inability to create it as such.

"That's not all," Leafy said as he bowed his head. "But first, we need to wait a while, and be very sure that they have left."

Lily and the children waited several minutes until they were certain the fishermen had gone, and then they crept along the shoreline.

As they reached the edge of the broken boat, the smell of dried, rotting fish overtook the fresh air. Lily felt sick from the smell of it. The children told Lily to peek over the edge. But Lily wished that she hadn't. For there, held by a net on the edge of the ship, was a pool of swimming mermaids and mermen, squashed in between each other, unable to move. Just silently crying. Lily made eye contact with one of them. But his eyes held no emotion. There was nothing left behind them. His energy had depleted trying to survive, trying to escape. Lily crept back down to the children.

"We have to save them. We have to release them!"

The children all shook their heads sadly.

"See that eagle?" Airlie pointed to a giant eagle that was perched in the top branch of a tall tree near the broken ship.

Lily nodded.

"Its eyes are seen from Queen Allura. If anyone tries to cut open this trap, she knows. And she knows who we are. We are told that if we do anything, that eagle will hunt us down" Leafy said as he led the way back toward the forest.

"I'm going to fix this!" Lily said angrily, nodding her head as the four began to walk back toward their home.

Lily could feel the disturbance in the energy between the children, and rightly so. It was such an awful sight for them to have witnessed. And the children were far too young to have seen such pain and misery inflicted from one person to another. As Lily walked with the children, she hated herself. Hated herself for what she had done. What kind of life she had created. It was because of her that the mermaids were discovered, and it was the worst thing that could have ever happened to the world of Sa Neo.

"I feel terrible about this," Lily said as she followed the children back toward the house.

"It's okay, it's not your fault," Oceana said, as she soothed Lily.

But Lily couldn't help but believe that it was. They didn't know who she really was. And she wanted so badly to tell them. But she just couldn't risk being hated for what had happened. Lily already hated herself for the past and she walked with great regret, heavy as the burden on her shoulders.

No one said a word as they walked back home. The sadness that had played out was still very present in their minds. Even though they had walked far away from it. It was still happening. And the memory of that small merchild's eyes was still alive in Lily's mind. She couldn't shake it. That little boy didn't deserve to be captured for someone's fun. He still had a long life in front of him. Lily could feel tears beginning to well in her eyes, but she fought them back. She needed to be strong in front of the children.

"What happens now?" Lily asked, as they walked into the backyard of the Marlina Residence.

"The ceremony of the moons takes place at nightfall," Leafy said. "We will meet around the bonfire."

seven

Three Full Moons

Lily, Marlina, Oceana, Leafy, and Airlie all walked through the center of the village as the nighttime began to fall. The stars gleamed brightly above, showcasing a wondrous display of beauty. But it wasn't only the stars that created such a magical show, for high above them shone three full moons. The moons hung low to the land, as though they weighed down heavily, bursting with light and electrical energy. They appeared to hang so close that Lily could see the craters carved on the surface of the moons. The craters were carved out like drawings, beautiful shapes and objects illustrated in perfect symmetry. They reminded Lily of cave drawings she once studied in school, and she stared at them with enchantment, wondering what message was being shown. And the longer she stared at the moons, the more they continued to change. The shapes turned into people, lands, rivers, and faces. Right before her eyes. As though the moons were trying to tell Lily a story.

The sound of drums beating could be heard in the far distance, and it purred through the air like a cat calling its prey. A rhythmic tone that hypnotized the village people, pulling them closer to the great ceremony. Sparks of fire erupted high above the trees, and the smell of burning ashes seeped through the woods. Before long, they had arrived to an open space of land, where a giant bonfire was blazing high in the center. It was the biggest fire Lily had ever seen, and she stood frozen, bewitched with the licking flames of purple, white and orange. She wondered how such beauty could be capable of creating a mass destruction.

Around the fire danced a stream of beautiful women and men, half clothed, half naked, dancing in wild movements and shaking their body as though they were possessed by a strange magic. With flowers in their hair and musical instruments in hand, they chanted together, moving and swaying in fast and slow motion. Those who jilted in rhythmic paces vibrated quickly, and some even levitated off the ground. And those who moved in slow vibrations held a shadow self who cooed gently behind them, a stream of auric energy protecting them from one another, and yet within their own bubble they were free to play as they so wished. To the sides of the dancing sat little workshops. In one, a lady was painting the faces of children and women, colorful paints of all shades. Some faces were drawn like tigers, small and thick stripes, and others were shapes so complex they appeared to be hieroglyphs, speaking words upon their skin. Next to the painting ladies sat five older women creating a potion. They had taken plants and were burning them beneath a large old oven. It was a dugout hole of dirt and coals, with leaves and wood pressed over it, with a giant cauldron pot hanging over a smaller fire. With their bare hands they mixed the finished potion, spinning the fluid around and around, cooking it carefully over the fire.

Many animals had also gathered to watch the party. Panthers, wolves, and bears all stood by and watched. They would run into the center at times, stretching their claws, rolling on the ground, or growling. The owls in the trees hooted, and the bats overhead flew near. As the fire cackled with great strength, the sparks bursting so high into the air, it appeared as though it touched the moon, and graced the stars above. And the sparks burst overhead, showering the village folk with glitter.

Two younger men dressed in pale-orange pants sat with very loud drums, and they beat them with great strength. And with one final clash of their hands, the music ceased with no sound at all.

"Quickly, bow down," Marlina instructed to Lily and the children, as they all crouched and bowed their heads.

"That's Queen Allura," Airlie whispered to Lily, pointing to a lady in the opposite corner of the fire.

Queen Allura wore a crown of the finest orange crystals Lily had ever seen. It was delicately created with thin gold stars and triangles. The crown sat proudly on top of her hair, which was bright orange, wild, and luscious. She wore a long gold-chained dress, which linked together in tiny triangles; it covered her body right down to the ground. And around her neck she caressed a thick orange snake, whose body wrapped around Allura's stomach, and the snake's head rested just beside her chin.

"My beautiful friends, it is ready," the Queen said as she walked around the center of the fire.

The elderly ladies who were making the potion carried the large cauldron toward her, and the village folk all picked up their painted clay cups, ready to share the magical potion.

"My fellow family from the land of Praza," Allura continued, as she looked over her shoulders from left to right, smiling, with her eyes half closed. "Tonight we celebrate the magic from our ancestors. Tonight we shed the blood from our truth."

The village folk moved in closer to Allura and they stared with open mouths, hanging longingly on her every word.

"Today we celebrate the story of what has been. The life that was taken as a sacrifice to all of our kind. We remember," Allura said as she continued to circle the fire.

"We remember," the village folk chanted in response.

"Many, many moons ago, Queen Jade from the Land of Tehar shared this world with us," Allura said as she stopped in front of the children and raised her arms.

Lily's body twitched with terror as the memory of Queen Jade flashed back into her mind and she tapped her fingers together quickly, trying to release the nervous energy. But the image of Jade stood strong, no matter how she tried to shake it. And the vision of evil overclouded her thoughts, freezing her body and forcing her to forget where she was and what she was doing.

"But a strange girl from a faraway galaxy brought great shame to our future," Allura continued, leaning close to the children, making sure they could hear. Lily shook back to life as she looked around at the village folk, realizing that Allura was speaking about her. Lily squirmed and looked to Marlina and the children. They were all looking at Lily with no expression on their faces.

"It was from this girl that we learned of the evil that existed beneath the waters. That beneath our own feet bore creatures that were more powerful in many ways than we could ever be. They brought terror to our lands, and threatened our survival."

Allura waved her hand to the fire, as it cast a great explosion of smoke above them upon which a story played out in animation. It was the image of a mermaid and a witch at war.

"But we are smarter, and much stronger than they realized," she continued. "One day, a merman lured one of Jade's workers into the ocean, to capture her for his own pleasure. Upon hearing news of such a tragedy, Jade rushed to save her own people. She cared greatly of her land and of every witch, fairy, and creature who lived there."

The village folk nodded in agreement, and an overall feeling of safety washed over their beings, realizing that they, too, were fortunate to be protected by a leader who had their best interests at heart.

"But when the courageous Queen Jade walked to the ocean, the merman was too powerful, and too strong and too wicked; he pierced an arrow of death with just one look from his eyes, and instantly, the beloved Queen Jade had died."

"Ooooh," sighed the village folk as a puff of smoke from the fire displayed Queen Jade and the ghastly death. They all coughed as they cried, as though in a sympathetic tone. But Lily felt as though it was a warning from Allura, showing that she was the one with the power, and that death could soon be upon them.

"How can we live in safety?" one of the village folk jumped up and cried out, asking for mercy from the Queen.

"We must destroy the mermaids!" Allura announced as a thunderous roar from the crowd clapped in support. "Now, let us unite together and dance in peace, and sing our strength to intimidate, and drink to awaken the creativity that lies dormant within us!"

The music grew louder as the magic potion from the caldron was poured out into the triangular cups.

"Te Te Hara Te! Ci Te Si Te Mi Te!" the village folk chanted as they drank the potion together.

In an instant, their bodies had changed into a different form. Some had slumped over into awkward shapes as though their bodies were too heavy for them. It was as though their Soul had forgotten what it was like to live in a body, and they danced up high above in the galaxy. With wide eyes and slow motions, they appeared to be in a zombie-like state within their own skin. Others had laid down to rest, pointing to the sky and the stars as though reading messages from above. Queen Allura sat back on her throne, out of the light and into the shadows, watching everyone carefully from afar.

Lily felt scared. The story was about her; she knew it. If she was found out, she didn't know what they would do. Yet at the same time she wanted to yell that the story didn't happen that way. She ached for the truth to be told. For everyone to know that the mermaids had beautiful souls with pure intentions, that they were curious and playful creatures. But the history had been changed by the Queen so that her people would live in fear. *Why create such an unnecessary flood of terror in their lives?* Lily wondered. The Queen was not only allowing fear to take over all rationality, she was encouraging it. She was using fear as a way for her to hold power, a way to make the people do whatever she wished them to do. It was a tragedy, for now the truth lay buried beneath the ground, along with the ancestors, unable to be recovered.

"To the Gods of the Sun, the Moon, the Thunder and Lightning. Look after us. Accept this sacrifice of our loyalty, our gratitude and love," the Queen said, as the three fishermen walked into the circle from the bushes holding a long piece of wood and carrying the young mermaid who Lily had seen captured earlier that day. The scales of the mermaid were no longer vibrant and gleaming, they had changed into an off white, and her hair hung over the edges of the wooden plank like lifeless strings. Her eyes were open slightly and Lily felt as though they were staring directly at her. As the two connected together Lily felt a wave of electricity jolt through her body, as though she could feel the mermaid's heart beating. Despite the noise of the music and the people around her, Lily could feel that the mermaid was still alive. Lily felt dizzy, her head was itchy and hot, and her whole body began to shake in outrage. She wanted to stand up and yell that the mermaid was a living creature, and that alone demanded the same respect as anyone else. But she couldn't do it. Fear overtook all rationality. And so she watched, with silent tears.

"Everyone look at this treasure we have caught today," Queen Allura said as she touched the wrist of the mermaid. "Our ancestors have given us a gift for our full moons' ceremony."

Lily looked to the children who had all turned away from Allura and were cuddling in closely. Marlina was trying to convince them to turn their heads back, but to look elsewhere.

"She will know if you don't look," Marlina whispered, as she squeezed Airlie's hand tightly, telling her to look at the full moons.

Lily hated that the children were forced to watch such evil play out, she knew the truth from their hearts and their eyes—they did not wish death upon anyone.

"This creature is a gift for you, my Gods. All we ask is for your blessing in return," Queen Allura commanded, as the two men threw the mermaid onto the giant bonfire.

A deafening echo of screams shrieked from beneath the ocean, and the wolves amongst the land howled into the air too.

Lily's heart bled to watch the mermaid in such agony. *No wonder Indigo hates me,* Lily thought, as now slowly everything made sense to her. But what had become of this world? What was once the most joyous place had now turned to anger, power, and greed. Tears from Lily's eyes dripped down along her cheeks, and she wept quietly on her own. Realizing that her greatest fear had entwined its way into her reality—her actions had destroyed their innocent world.

"Leave." Lily heard a voice inside her heart say, as she looked down to wipe away the tears from her face.

"You!" shouted Queen Allura, as she appeared before Lily, towering over her. "Why do you cry?"

Her brilliant mane of orange hair moved gently in the wind, and the crown was even more incredible up close. Energetic colors from the crown hovered like smoke around Allura's face, and the power that she possessed was intoxicating. Lily thought to herself that Allura was the most beautiful Queen she had ever seen. Her face held strong characteristics—thick, luscious lips and a bold nose. Her eyes were completely black, but the edges were painted with orange dots like a speckled egg.

"Who are you?" the Queen asked as she poked Lily with a long wand covered in orange crystals.

"She's our cousin, visiting from Naja," Marlina said as she stood up and smiled at Allura.

"Why doesn't she talk for herself?" Queen Allura asked as she pointed the stick hard into Lily's chest, motioning for her to stand up. "Let us see if you are telling the truth."

Lily tried to speak, but her mouth wobbled, and as she tried to open her mouth, no words came out; she felt as though her mouth was tied shut. Her heart started to beat faster and droplets of sweat from the heat of the fire surfaced on her back. She felt giddy. The aroma of the potion that whirled around them was overpoweringly strong and Lily breathed slowly, easing herself into the moment of what she was being presented with. "Take your time," a voice said inside. "RUN!" said another.

The children were all looking at Lily with horror on their faces: Airlie was crying, Leafy held his hands in prayer, and Oceana looked down, terrified.

"I believe you might be a gift from the moons tonight," the Queen said as she blinked her eyes hurriedly. "Come with me." Her voice trailed off as she took a large step forward, pushing the stick harder into Lily's chest. Lily had no other option but to walk toward the fire. She could feel the heat from the fire grow fiercely as each step brought her closer. The music came to a halt as Lily's presence came into vision for all to see, and the women and children stopped dancing, waiting for Allura's command.

"I believe this unknown girl has been brought to us from the heavens above," the Queen said as she hushed the crowd quietly. "For she cannot tell me who she herself is, let us ask the Gods and see if they grant her safety."

The village folk around the fire began to laugh as they pointed at Lily. Lily felt her lips, and they were exactly as she thought, sealed shut from a bamboo straw woven through her skin. Tears pierced down her cheeks as she looked to the others for help. But no one dared to move.

"Know your place here with us. We don't welcome strangers lightly," the Queen continued as she pointed to a tiger on her right who immediately came over and guarded Lily.

Lily's heart raced in an abnormal heartbeat. It skipped all over the place, starting with a strong first beat, and then a fast pace then back to one single slow beat. As she stood amongst the staring witches she only wished one thing: that she had never visited Sa Neo again. Why was she so stupid? There had been no good to come of it so far, she was constantly faced with a dark shadow of herself. A dark shadow of what she had done. *Or has the shadow always been here with me, and this land has just magnified it into light?* she wondered.

The tiger started to walk closely behind Lily, prompting her to move toward the fire. And with each step that Lily took, layers of confusion peeled from her mind. She stared, pleading with the empty faces of the beautiful creatures that lined the pathway. They all appeared so innocent, so pure and willing to follow the Queen's commands, wanting to fit in. Lily could feel that they didn't know who they really were themselves. They hadn't spent the time getting to know about their own Soul, and so instead, they allowed a leader to take control for them. To be told as cattle what it was that they were to do. And right now, if the Queen was to say that Lily was their enemy, then they would obey, no questions asked.

"Queen Allura," came the voice of a tall man with a dark orange apron and a pointy beard. "I'm sorry to interrupt, but it's ready."

"Not now!" Allura shook her head angrily at the man.

"I'm sorry, Queen Allura, but if you don't come now, it won't be until the next full moons." The tall man bowed his head, nervous for the interruption, but at the same time he was confident he had done the right thing.

"Okay," Allura replied, nodding her head and following the man. "Tie the girl up until I return and bring her next to me so I can keep a close eye on her."

Allura walked back to a lavish bed full of plush pillows and orange silk sheets. Lily followed with two men restraining her movements, and they tied her up with a piece of rope around her ankles.

"Wait here," Allura instructed as she sat on the bed, propping herself up against the pillows.

The man with the apron appeared once more, holding a large wooden tray with a fish tail on it. The flesh of the fish was cooked thoroughly and Lily felt sick as she stared at the piece of meat, realizing it was the mermaid's tail.

"Thank you for this gift," Allura said to the chef, as she gazed with excitement over the cooked piece of fish.

But Lily felt ready to vomit. The fish they were referring to was a real living creature. She wanted to scream. That piece of meat once had a heart, and she was loved. She had a life, a happy one. And then one day, someone higher up in the hierarchy decided that they were hungry, and that the small petite mermaid would make a fine meal for them. But it wasn't food. It was murder! Lily's body began to shake with anger. Not only were the village folk capturing these creatures, they were eating them too.

"May you have a safe journey," the man replied, as he handed Allura a cup of the potion that everyone was drinking.

Allura took a deep breath in and muttered something quietly under her breath. She poured the potion over the mermaid's tail, closed her eyes, and took a large bite.

But as Allura ate the tail and drank the potion, she appeared to react differently to the other village folk. She lay heavily on the cushions as her eyes sank back into her head. She appeared to have fallen into a deep dark sleep.

"Leave." a voice inside of Lily screamed loudly again.

It was a kick inside her chest that pushed her to move, and Lily thought of the only thing she could do—transport to another land as she was taught once before.

The crowd around was dancing and singing loudly. Even the guards appeared to be drunk on the magical potion. And so, in very small movements, Lily subtly crept her hand into her pouch, grasping the closest crystal she could find. She needed to leave this land as quickly as possible. The surface of the stone was engraved in Lily's mind. She had touched those crystals a million times before. Through her classes when she was nervous, when playing in her room, and whenever she needed strength, she found herself holding her crystals for positivity. She looked after her crystals too, the same way she was taught. Wash the crystals in sea salt and on every full moon, lay them out to recharge, reenergize. Lily was holding the purple-colored amethyst, which was from the seventh land of Neveah, where Violetta, the most powerful Empress of Sa Neo, lived. Lily knew it was no coincidence, that the opening to see Violetta landed at the right time, again as usual.

Lily cleared her mind, erasing out any thoughts of fear or trauma that had entered. She knew the situation she was in was heartbreakingly freaky. It held the ability to destroy her, but there was another way, a better way. And she knew she could take herself there, if she just focused on clearing her mind. Careful not to draw too much attention to herself, she envisioned the snow-kissed land of Neveah, and thought about the chilly temperatures, the polar bears, and the white flowers. "Take me to Neveah," she chanted in her head, repeating the words in a mantra. Over and over again. And as she looked at Queen Allura's face one last time, she closed her eyes, praying, pleading, but most importantly envisioning that she had already departed and was standing on the frozen shores of Neveah.

eight

The Pilgrimage

Lily sighed with relief as she opened her eyes to the mystical land of Neveah. The snow covered the ground like a thick fluffy blanket, and as Lily stood on the shores of the freezing cold beach, she could feel the prickles of water flush over her stance. They flew from the ocean to where she stood and she moved quickly away from the winter splinters. The sun had now come into full view, as the land she now stood on was on the opposite side of the world. In an instant, with one thought, she kissed the amethyst crystal in her hand, thanking it for pulling her through and abiding with her wishes. The mountains lay in the far horizon, and the howling wind kissed Lily's cheeks in small breaths of fresh air. Lily's clothes had doubled in thickness and in size. No longer was she wearing her floral printed dress, she was now covered from head to toe in a warm, cuddly jumpsuit and purple gumboots. The edges of Lily's sleeves had miniature teardrops of amethyst crystals on them, and as Lily moved her arms, she could hear them twinkle lightly together.

Lily was standing next to a tall tree that had frozen droplets of ice decorating its arms—they looked like tiny snow petals. Tiny white flowers tickled the tips of the branches, allowing a sweet aroma of jasmine to waft through the space. Lily could hear the sound of an angelic harp playing nearby and as she turned around, there sat an exquisite woman on a clear crystal throne. The woman wore a long gown of purple lace, woven with gold thread, creating a pattern of diamond shapes. Her silver hair flowed in curls, reaching past the harp and down to the edge of her dress, which spread out around her in a large circle. She appeared to have taken no notice of the cold, for she exhaled easily with radiance, as though the air refreshed her with new energy, and new vibrations. Her fingernails were painted a soft purple and they were pointed with sharp tips. She wore a ring on each finger, connecting them together, and it was attached with a chain around her wrist. Another gold chain rested easily upon her head, which matched the jewelry on her hands, and by either side of her ear lay a small diamond-shaped amethyst crystal. The golden chains hung down low as well, and she appeared like a fashionable piece of artwork, a delicate display that concealed her true self. She looked far into the horizon, as opposed to the instrument that was creating the peaceful melody. And in between her long, drawn-out breaths she would close her eyes, living purely in the moment, allowing herself to be mesmerized by her own enchanting beauty.

Lily walked closer to the lady as she searched through her bag for an offering of peace. Lily pulled out the small twig of rosemary leaves. The smell reminded her of her garden, a place that she found peace within herself when she would visit. How little understanding she used to have of Mother Nature's gifts. How once upon a time she would play in the garden and not realize how blessed her life really was. Lily stood next to the lady, careful not to disturb her song until she finished. Lily knew that there was nothing worse than being interrupted in the middle of creativity. When those moments of inspiration tapped through one's Soul it needed to be acted upon immediately, for when doing so, allowed the beholder to experience a euphoric bliss. The lady finished her song with a long, humming noise, and as she did so a flock of birds flew overhead, as though they had been listening for many hours and needed to continue on their journey.

The lady placed her hands on her lap and looked to Lily, still, in slow motion. She opened her eyes wide, showing a diamond-shaped deep-purple pupil in the center. Her eyelashes swept across her face from the far edges of each eye, and she smiled, childlike, as though she had discovered a new friend to play with.

"I brought this gift for you," Lily said as she handed the lady a handful of rosemary leaves.

The lady held her hand out to receive the gift. As she took hold of the leaves, a fire blasted from her palm, burning the rosemary leaves up into flames, releasing a sweet-smelling perfume.

"What a beautiful gift," the lady said as she inhaled the smoke, rolling her eyes back in an exhilarated state of pleasure.

"You're very welcome," Lily replied, smiling sweetly at the lady. "My name is Lily. I have journeyed far to visit Violetta."

The lady turned her head and looked out to the sea, as though in grieving memory of what was, once upon a time.

"No one has seen her for many moons," the lady replied, pulling a small bottle from the ground and pouring an oil over her hands. "Some say she has traveled through the mountains. Others say she has gone to the underworld."

"What do you believe?" Lily asked, noticing how the oil lathered up and soaked the golden chains and rings on her fingers, making the gold sparkle brightly.

"I think it is sad that we are at war," the lady replied quietly. As she spoke, a single tear of golden dew dripped down her face and trailed a long line, dropping perfectly on her dress and staining a hole.

Lily nodded in agreement. She too was devastated that the world was at war. The witches against the mermaids, and it was clear the mermaids were losing drastically.

"Which mountains do they say Violetta resides in?" Lily asked, staring at the snowy mountains that stood behind them.

"She is said to be at the top of the mountain that looks like an elephant."

The lady pointed to the largest mountain in the far distance that overhung the ocean.

"How far do you think it is?" Lily asked as she turned back around to the beautiful lady.

But the lady had frozen into a statue. She now appeared as a stone etching, cold as the snow, and her imagery of being alive ceased to exist at all. The gold chains, the purple dress. It was all painted meticulously onto the lady. Her arms had risen once again to play the golden harp that sat before her. And through the air Lily could hear her soft hum, the sound of the harp playing still, somewhere far away.

Lily was used to things changing quickly in Sa Neo, especially in Neveah compared to the other lands. There was no predictability to Nevaeh, it was by far the most magical and mystical. She was surrounded by a world that displayed not only what she chose to see, but what she needed to see. Her filter of what she chose to perceive was being tested and her intuitive guidance was loud and clear. For now, Lily picked up on the signs. She knew the direction, and the purpose she needed to pursue. She wondered if her life back home was like that too. If she was constantly provided with hints of her true path, perhaps she just wasn't paying attention. But like the lady turning to stone, once the message had been heard, it would go away.

The elephant-shaped mountain appeared quite far away, and Lily didn't know any magic that could help transport her faster. *At least I am safe in Neveah,* she thought. A small pathway of amethyst crystals revealed itself to Lily as she ventured toward the mountains and she thought about her displacement as she trekked. The first time she visited Sa Neo was short-lived and yet somehow it had impacted her mind frame for the next several years after. *How strange that one tiny experience can do that,* she thought. But although her footprints were deleted as soon they existed, it was apparent that her ideas and energy had remained upon the land, the change that she had ignited from walking her path before. She realized that it made sense for her to now come back at a time when the war was at its peak.

And so Lily followed the path high up above the snowy mountain tops, and in between bridges that enabled safe passage across ice lakes. Through her adventures in the snow she admired a different kind of beauty from Mother Nature. Before, she would stare at the miniature creations, the flowers, the trees, the dirt and the insects. Here, she marveled at the vast land that stretched out for miles, and emptied her thoughts upon the simplicity of white snow against the bright purple sky. There was a true sense of liveliness around her. It was as though she could feel a heart beating from inside the core of the world, and it bounced up in vibrations through the ground (which was like its skin). A protective layer that displayed such beauty, with trees and mountains decorating the unique imperfections of a body. It was more powerful than any person, any magic, anything. It simply was, just by being. And yet the most miraculous truth of it all, it was existing and non-existing at the same time—constantly bouncing between Lily's perception, and a galactic world of stardust.

The backdrop of Neveah was so expansive that as Lily stared at it, she felt completely insignificant. It reminded her that she could disappear and no one would know. *But to do such a thing would be selfish,* Lily thought. She knew that there were others suffering and she couldn't ignore the plea for help. She needed to make a change in their world, a change that would shift their future and the course of history. All it took was just one person to stand up for what was ethically right.

And so, Lily continued to walk. The sun had begun to lower itself into the horizon, disappearing from the world. Lily liked to think that perhaps the sun fell into the ocean, so that the mermaids had their time with the brilliant star too. She knew that the night sky meant it would be time to rest soon, and she hoped that she would be able to find a small cottage, or even an area to stay warm for a few hours. But she had never seen a village or even houses in Neveah, and she started to feel a little worried about what would happen next.

She had so many questions in her head about surviving the mountains by herself. What kind of animals lived in Neveah? Would she be too cold to last the night? But the fears didn't waver her determination, she knew what she needed to do. She had to surrender to the situation, allow the universe to lay a path out before her. But a part of her held a small dose of fear, wondering if the universe really was looking after her after all. Or was this her punishment for what she had done? Was this the hand of karma finally playing its part?

"Dear Heavens above, please guide me on my journey. Please walk me to safety, to Violetta, and to save this beautiful world." Lily recited the prayer in her mind as she continued on her journey. Immediately after Lily spoke her prayer she saw in the far distance some smoke drifting through the air from the ground, suggesting there could be a fire burning, a place to get some warmth. As Lily walked closer, she realized that it wasn't a cottage, but an igloo-shaped home made out of glass. Next to the igloo was an open fire, with a small, gnome-looking man roasting potatoes that were buried in the coals. The gnome was dressed in a balloon-cushioned jumpsuit and he wore a purple hat on his head. His nose protruded loudly from his face, with a pointed red tip as though he was too cold.

Lily watched the gnome for several minutes before interrupting. He was a jolly fellow, toasting the potatoes and talking to them.

"Now you, little leftie, I'd like you to crisp up like old ranger here. What's that, shortie? Yes, me thinks you're quite ready," he mumbled, giggling to himself and patting his knee.

"Hello, there," Lily said as she entered the space of the gnome. "May I join you?"

"Hello, beautiful girl!" the gnome said as he stood up, smiling. He reached no taller than Lily's knee and bowed down proudly, taking off his small hat to reveal a bald head. "Of course, I'd be honored. Come, come here," he said as he pointed to a cushioned rug he had been sitting on. And he went into the igloo to bring back another cushion, which he placed near her.

"Can I offer you something to eats?" he asked as he proudly displayed his baked potatoes in the fire.

"Yes, please that would be wonderful," Lily replied, feeling happy in herself for finding him and she quietly said a little prayer to the Universal Energies with gratitude for guiding her to him. "My name is Lily."

"Nice to meet you, Lily. Just call me Arra. My name's the same backward as it is forward—there're no secrets here! Ha ha ha!" He laughed as he placed three roasted potatoes on a ceramic plate. "I mean, what more could you want from life? I have a fire to give me warmth and the stars above my head! Ha ha ha!" He laughed again as he pulled out seasoning and sprinkled it generously over the plate of potatoes.

"Thank you so much," Lily replied, taking the plate and breaking the potato apart with her hand.

The exterior of the skin cracked open effortlessly, as though aching to be broken, and the inside of the potato was soft and fluffy.

"Oh, wait!" Arra waved his hand in front of Lily, stopping her from taking a bite. "Would you like the special ingredient?" Arra asked as his eyes opened wide, displaying a bright yellow hue, and he raised his eyebrows as he held a tiny jar.

"What is it?" Lily nodded with equal enthusiasm; it was difficult not to be excited.

"Well, let me tell you about it first. I traveled to the land of Deia —you know, the fifth land of Sa Neo—just to get them."

"You did?"

"Oh, it was well worth it though," Arra replied with a great big sigh, signaling that he had endured a difficult journey to obtain the secret ingredient.

"And what did you get?" Lily asked, intrigued to hear what the secret ingredient was.

"Qurata herbs!" Arra said as he proudly displayed the tiny jar in front of Lily. "Oh, they simply are THE most marvelous flavor you could ever possibly imagine! It's the little things in life that makes you happy, you know?"

He winked again as he carefully took the lid off the bottle. As soon as he did the most incredible smell drifted through the air. It made Lily's mouth water, even though she had never tried the herbs before.

"Just a little touch of this Jarina oil and the Qurata herbs and oh, Lily, this is living you know. Ha ha ha!" Arra laughed again as he dressed the potatoes with a touch of oil. "Go on, take a bite now," he encouraged as he stood up close to Lily's mouth.

He only stood as tall as Lily was sitting down, and he hovered over her and her food, too eager to witness her reaction.

"Oh, it's simply scrumptious, however did you know about the Qurata herbs?"

"Oh, everyone knows about the Qurata!" Arra slapped his knee as he sat down on his cushion, filling his own plate up with potatoes. "It's how you find them that makes it difficult. They only grow on the very top of the Qurata tree you see. And these trees are so tall, only the flying folk can get them. So you see, me first went to the land of Salor, that's where the best dragonflies are, then me flew all over the ocean to Deia, and up to the topmost tree."

Arra nodded his head as he used his hands to show the size of the tree. "Me made a deal with the dragonfly, you see: I gets half, he gets half. Even shares, I am," Arra explained as he tipped small sprinkles of the Qurata herbs on his potatoes.

Lily loved listening to Arra tell his story. She couldn't help but admire the simplicity of his pleasures. Good food in his stomach, and the world at his feet. He knew exactly what it was that made him happy. *What a blessed life,* she thought.

"So what are you doing in this world?" Arra asked, taking a big bite of the golden, crispy potato.

"How did you know that I'm not from Sa Neo?"

"I know I'm not much to the eye, but I've been around long enough, I gots a sense for these things." Arra winked again. "Plus, not many village folk live in Neveah."

"Yes, why is that?" Lily asked, taking a bite of the fluffy potato, thinking about how delicious the oil was.

"Maybe the weather? Ha ha ha." He laughed again. "I love it here. Feeling warm inside and cold on the outside. Plus me in my little igloo, no one bothers me. It's me and all me. And I'm the happiest I could ever be! Ha ha ha."

Lily looked to the igloo and smiled. It certainly looked cozy and well maintained. For such a tiny space he had managed to squeeze every necessity into perfection. There was a little bed with a nightstand where a small book sat. Next to the bed was a beautiful bathtub, and along the circumference further was a comfortable couch and table. It all flowed in one long symmetry, around in a spiral. And directly in the center was a cushioned circle with a giant pillow.

"You are right, your home certainly looks comfortable."

"You're welcome to stays you know. Have you ever stayed in such a beautiful place? Waking up to the sounds of nature all around?"

"No, never," Lily replied, wondering why she never had camped outside before.

"You can take my bed. I like to sleep outside every now and again. It keeps me on me toes. Plus, look at this view!" he said as he pointed up to the beautiful star-filled sky.

The stars twinkled like a smashed mirror thrown over a black canvas, and it illuminated from the sun shining from beneath the underworld.

Lily smiled. She forgot how incredibly beautiful the night sky was in Sa Neo, and in the world of Neveah, it appeared even more incredible. The three moons weighed heavily in the sky; they appeared more vibrant than the land of Praza.

"Your life looks wonderful. But do you not have any family to share this with?" Lily asked, although she immediately wished she didn't. For the look on Arra's face changed to the saddest she had ever seen. All the wrinkles on his face that curved upward to his smile flattened hard on his skin, and he looked down, deep in thought.

"I had a family, I did," he finally said, still unable to look at Lily.

"It's okay, if you don't want to talk about it, I'm sorry to have brought it up."

"No, it's good to talk about it, me thinks. No secrets. You know? That's how we all got into this mess," Arra said as his stood up and walked over to Lily, nodding to himself as though he needed to let his story breathe. "I had a little girl, but I wasn't a good father to her, because ...well, my father gave me this." Arra leaned in close to the fire, showing Lily the edge of a dotted line tattoo just next to his ear. But the rest of his skin he had burned slightly. "It wasn't my fault. I know that now. Not that I blame me parents, but well, they didn't heal you see. They passed on the pain, and so I did what I thought was best. But now, it's too late to fix it. I don't know where she is." Arra pulled out a small flask from his pocket and took a swig. He handed it to Lily who politely declined. "This is the real reason why I wander this world. It's not just about food you see; well, it helps the day pass by. But part of me is looking for her. And the other part, is escaping her, unable to stand up for my responsibilities still."

"I'm sorry," Lily said, nodding empathetically. "That's why I'm here, in Neveah. I'm trying to find Violetta and help stop Allura from spreading this evil."

"Well, I'm no Violetta, but I can tell you what I've learned on the road all this time." Arra sat back down now and pulled out a stick to poke the fire. "No one is born evil. It's the result of a pain inherited from those who'd passed. People inflict hurt on each other so they don't have to deal with the pain inside of themselves. Well that's what me thinks. When they show you acts of hate, it's because deep within there's an absence of love." Arra spoke clearly, as though these thoughts had played over in his mind for many years.

"Arra you're right." Lily nodded, surprised with the wisdom of the funny little man. "So, how can we help those who are misled? Those who are foolishly following Allura's way of life?"

"Well, you need to understand how they gots there in the first place," Arra replied as he stood up, and cleared his throat, signaling a stance of importance. "Allura befriended them at a time in their life when they had no one who loved or understood them. And instead of being that someone themselves, they allowed another to take on that responsibility. They lack love themselves. They don't know their own value. So, she's smart that Allura. She sees an opportunity and she takes it! She provides a sense of worth, gives them a purpose in life and provides a support network, handing it out as a generic formula, yet they feel they are the only one. It's not their fault, because they don't know any different. They just haven't spent time getting to know themselves. Do you know what I mean?"

As Arra spoke Lily reflected on his words; it was clear that he had delved deep within his own actions over the many years that he journeyed on the road. For although he was speaking advice on others, the words he shared were really to himself.

"How do we change their mind?"

"Well. Me thinks we have to show them the love they never got. We needs to forgive them. They're just reacting to fear of themselves and their life, and they're repeating the cycle because they don't know how to get out of it. Most of these cycles have been in repetition for thousands of generations. And they are simply playing their part forward, pushing their lack of self-love onto their children and the next children after that. They want a way out but they don't know how." The words that Arra spoke flew through his mouth like a constant stream of water. It just didn't stop. And it didn't sound like him, it was as though he was channeling a higher entity, for his persona had calmed down to a minimum, and the wisdom in his words moved through effortlessly.

"It seems impossible to give that many people love though." Lily sighed; she felt dwarfed by such a task, and although she had no intention of giving up, it was easy to want to.

"Me thinks you will figure this out, don't worry." Arra smiled, handing Lily another potato.

"Well, I just hope I can find Violetta, maybe she will know. Do you know if there's a shortcut to Elephant Rock? It looks so far."

"I have just the thing." Arra nodded, and he tapped on the edge of his knee three times. "Come out now, don't be shy." Arra was speaking to a small animal behind a tree. And upon his command, a beautiful white-haired fox came forth with black-and-purple striped eyes. Arra was only half its size, and he reached up high on his toes to scratch behind the fox's ears.

"It looks like someone here wants to help you out. Ha ha ha." Arra laughed as he play-fought with the white fox. "Lily, meet Gria."

"I don't understand..." Lily said nervously as she looked at the fox.

"Didn't you want to see Violetta?" Arra asked, as he broke open a potato and handed it to the fox. "Gria here is happy to help you. She has a Soul like you and me. Tomorrow, after you've had a good night's rest, we'll tie a sleigh to her and she will carry you to Violetta. Simple really. Ha ha ha."

And Lily laughed too, a roaring laugh as deep as Arras. She couldn't believe it and yet at the same time she could, for her life was always timed perfectly when she made a decision to follow through with something. She set the intention, and the world around her responded. It was the universe agreeing and complimenting her with surprises, affirming her desires and matching the same vibrational frequency that she was emitting.

Lily slept very soundly that night in the glass shaped igloo under the stars, completely surrounded by nature. The harmonious land felt very healing for everything Lily was going through. And before she went to sleep, she wished upon the three moons for guidance. She finally felt as though she had realized the solution to the problem, but it was a revolution that she needed to ignite, and she had no idea how to do that. All she wanted was for everything to change around her. As she got irritated with the lack of change, she realized that the advice that she was trying to give to others, she needed to give to herself. If she wanted the world to change, she needed to be the one who changed. And with that epiphany in her mind, Lily fell fast asleep.

nine

Parietal Art

Gria, the beautiful white fox, ran wild and free through the snowy mountains, pulling Lily upon the sleigh. After many hours they had finally arrived at the Elephant Rock. *What a long drawn out journey we have endured,* Lily thought, smiling to herself with gratitude of being gifted with Gria's help. Lily reached into her bag and pulled out an acorn. Lily wasn't sure if it was the enchantment of being back in Neveah, or perhaps she felt as though she was close to Violetta, but she felt strong in her magical powers. The witchcraft she had learned from her time before was blazing with strength inside of her, itching to be ignited. She placed the acorn in her left hand and then kissed the ring on her right hand softly, while envisioning the acorn to mold into a large bowl of delicious fruits, berries, and vegetables. Lily imagined electrical currents moving from the tip of her head down through her heart and out to her fingers. When she opened her eyes she held a bowl of blessings as a gift to the beautiful white creature that had carried her on this journey. She cuddled Gria and scratched her nose. As Gria devoured the fruits and vegetables, Lily tickled behind her ears and wiped the snow off her fur coat.

Lily and Gria had traveled exceptionally high. The view towered over the backdrop of the entire land of Neveah. Snow blanketed for miles, flooding out from the top of the mountain point to the far skirts of the edge until it collapsed into the sea. The land was a mixture of snow and streams of ice water in between. On the far opposite end to where Lily stood was another mountain as brilliant as the one she was standing on. It looked out to the other edge of the beach, as though it too protected the shores for what was to come.

As Lily focused her eyes the mountain, the pattern of streams and snow that blanketed the distance of land between was aligned in perfect symmetry. Each quarter mirrored the other, and it created a beautifully designed large snowflake. Perfectly drawn as though a painter had manipulated the land to be envisioned as such. *What a fantastic architect this world has,* Lily thought.

Lily picked up a giant stick of wood from the ground nearby and moved closer to the opening of the mountaintop. The raw stone opened to a thin doorway, sheltering off the snow that could blow inside. Lily ran her fingers along the wooden stick from the base to the tip and envisioned a desert, dry and warm, enabling the stick to become completely removed of any liquid.

"I call upon the fire from the center of this world. Grant me your blessing, your peace, and your creative flame," she said out loud as she struck the wood against the edge of the cave. An electrical bolt of fire pierced through the end of the wooden stick, creating a marvelous flaming torch in her hand to shed light upon the darkness. The sound of the fire igniting in her hand echoed throughout the cave.

"Hello," Lily called, hearing only the sound of echoing replies saying hello back.

But the space and time between one hello to another confused Lily for it sounded as though someone else was near her.

The temperature inside the cave was surprisingly warm, and the energy of space felt safe. The flame on the end of Lily's wooden stick grew in strength as it licked the air, illuminating the entire cave. She could now see that the cave extended through another doorway. But as she walked through she arrived to the final room, a large opening that looked over the sea side of the mountain. And Lily bowed her head sadly as she realized that Violetta was nowhere to be seen.

In the center of the room a glorious fire that blazed up high, exploding to the ceiling every so often. The edge of the fire was decorated with large black obsidian crystals, laid out around it in a circular grid. Lily placed her torch upon the open fire and walked to the opening edge of the mountain where the wall dropped down to the ocean. The seas below tossed and turned wildly, and they wrapped around the mountain edge with great pleasure, smashing themselves wholeheartedly in tiny pieces over the rock, creating loud noises as the water dispersed high into the air.

She turned back around to look at the cave. The energy from the fire felt too alive. Lily felt as though it held its own entity, as though it were a portal to another world below. She wondered if it could suck her through into another time frame, another universe, if she dared to jump. The fire erupted in gigantic explosions, touching the ceiling of the cave. As Lily followed the line of fire up high above, she discovered ancient drawings etched out onto the ceiling. She lay down on the ground to get a better look. Secretly, she loved feeling the uneven gravel beneath her body and how the little grains of dirt wriggled beneath her skin. The different textures soothed her, as though she felt her place finally amongst the rubble on the ground. She stared at the drawings, trying to make sense of what messages lay before her.

The drawing was of three witches, holding hands around a fire. With flowers in their hair, and three full moons up above. But the fire was a mirror image below, for although it flamed above to the witches, and the full moons, it also flamed below. As an opposite construction. The same as what was above the planet was identical to beneath. And on the opposite side of the fire was a galaxy of stars, a glimmering pathway with floating angelic babies encircling it. Around the drawing were many lines and arrows which all pointed back to Lily. They pointed back to where she was lying.

Where's Violetta? she wondered.

The drawings didn't seem to help her. But then she remembered, perhaps there was something more to be shown. Something that she didn't realize was needing to be explained. She stood up and followed the arrows. What appeared to be pointed toward her were in fact pointing toward the fire. Lily stood as close as possible to the fire, gazing deeply within the flames. The coals where the flames struck appeared to be coming out from deep inside the mountain. There was no floor, just an opening of hollow ground, as though the mountain seeped down through to the center of the world, bringing light upward. She examined the burning coals more closely. They didn't appear to hold heat, or look as though they even burned. Instead, the outer lines rolled around separate from the internal; it was as though they were an imaginary ball. Lily picked up the stick and poked at the circles. The stick went right through them!

Perhaps I was right, and this opening is real. Lily wondered as she looked above at the drawings again. She remembered what the lady with the harp had said, how Violetta had gone to the mountains and also to the underworld. Lily tried to push the obsidian crystals around the fire, and the same thing happened, the outline of the crystals disappeared too, allowing an opening to be presented. Lily played with the idea in her head. She was finally enjoying her life changing quickly; it made her feel alive and kept her moving forward. And right now, she was stuck. She had no lead on where to go. Karisma was gone, Jacques wasn't "there." She didn't even know how to find Silvia. She knew from the beginning of her trip that she needed to see Violetta, and this was the closest she had felt to finding her. She wasn't going to give up, not now, when she knew that life was all about taking risks. *Bring me to Violetta,* Lily wished in her mind, imagining what it would be like to see her again. She envisioned the image of her great beauty, her strong, powerful presence. And so, with Lily's ring placed securely on her finger, she looked at the fire one last time, closed her eyes, and jumped through.

ten

Xous — the Underworld

Lily fell completely through the fire, down a black hole of nothingness, as though the fire never existed in the first place. When Lily opened her eyes, she was surrounded with stars and twinkling galaxies. But she wasn't falling, she was floating, like a delicate balloon, just gradually drifting down until she landed upon a field of black-colored dirt.

"Welcome, Lily," came a voice from behind her.

Lily knew who it was before she even turned around. She could feel the energy of the powerful Empress tickle through the back of her neck and soothe the currents of her Soul's vibration. And when Lily looked to the voice, as expected, there in front of her stood Violetta.

Violetta's presence overflowed with wisdom and it demanded respect. She connected worlds between what was known and unknown, the seen and unseen. And she drifted peacefully, beautifully, and seamlessly between them all. Lily felt like she had known Violetta for millions of lifetimes before, and yet, at the same time, she believed that she didn't know her at all.

"Violetta! Hello ..." Lily said excitedly as she stood up to greet her. "I'm so happy to see you again."

Violetta held no emotion. She stood from afar, a strong stance, a powerful entity. Her black skin, rich and soft, and her eyes, a light purple, strongly contrasting against it. Her hair was long, white and pure, exactly the same as Lily remembered. Violetta was wearing a thin lining of black fabric against her body, and on her face lay tiny diamonds, perfectly framing her features.

"I see you all the time," Violetta replied, as she encircled her hands around, creating a ball that resembled the world. "Here," Violetta continued, "this is where you've been." The ball floated up in the air, spinning around to show Lily the world that she once came from.

The ball stopped to hover over Lily's home country and as it did so, it zoomed in quickly, showing Lily's world unto herself. Her home with her father, the walk to school, her classes. The days that she lived were in repeat, as though she were watching her own story play out in front of her. But for some reason, she felt a bit sad witnessing her life like that. It was one never-ending routine. Wake up, school, go to sleep. Spend time with her father and do a few things that she loved. But she could see all the times that she hesitated to take the risk beneath her, and how the path of her life seemed to revolve around one continuous circle. She waited so long to visit her friends in Sa Neo, and the moment it had begun was the moment that her life around her had changed. She could feel a new energy ignite in her Soul, and it rippled out in effects beneath her. The stagnant energy was nowhere to be seen because she did something new, something different.

"Yes," Lily replied, as the "world" Violetta had created disappeared.

"Why did you wait so long to return?" Violetta asked as explosions of fire burst through the space and encircled where they stood.

"I was scared of the truth," Lily confessed, feeling the heat from the walls of fire warm her face. "But I was told in a dream that I needed to come back here. It told me that Sa Neo needed my help."

"Yes." Violetta nodded, slowly lowering her purple eyes to Lily. "We heal our story while we sleep. We travel to other realms and heed the legends of our ancestors' time. Our reality is not just while we're awake." Violetta nodded, holding her hand out for Lily to take. "Come, there is more work for you to do."

Lily held Violetta's hand and walked alongside her. The softness of Violetta's skin felt like that of a tiny baby, smooth and gentle, like it had never been touched. The fire around the girls grew in strength, climbing high above their heads. As Lily looked up she saw that the sky above now appeared like water, hovering as though they were standing beneath a giant ocean, with a glass ceiling protecting them from the water falling down.

"Do you know why I am back?" Lily asked as Violetta guided her to sit down on a stone chair that appeared from the dirt ground.

"You are here to heal from your past," Violetta said as she twirled her finger around, creating an outline of another ball in midair. "This knowledge you seek to soothe your fears already resides within you, you are just ignoring it," Violetta continued as she reached up high, collecting a handful of water from above their heads. She tipped the water into the circle and it spun around turbulently. "We are here to remind you of what you already know," she said as she grasped a handful of fire and placed it inside the circle. "This great wisdom is embedded in you from lifetimes before."

Violetta picked up a small handful of dirt from the ground, adding it to the concoction of fire and water that was mixing together within the ball. And lastly, she blew air onto it very gently as the four elements rotated within, each separated with their own entity, each defined and visible as they complemented each other beautifully. Violetta held the ball lightly as she turned it around and around. The diamonds on her face shone brightly as she did so, changing color as the ball rotated. The ball stopped spinning, and Violetta opened her eyes. The purple within them twinkled loudly. And as she blinked, a spark of lightning appeared. It stayed strong, in manifested form. Violetta lifted the lightning spark in the air and placed it inside the center of the ball. It ignited a great explosion which eliminated all blackness within the atmosphere. And when the light subsided, there Violetta stood, holding a baby.

The baby lay perfectly still on Violetta's palm with closed eyes. She kissed the child on its head, whispered into its ear and then threw it high up through the sky, through the water, and beyond what the eye could see.

Violetta smiled and looked to Lily. It was the first time Violetta had ever smiled at Lily, and it was a strange feeling. Her smile encompassed mystery of her wisdom, and who she was. Yet at the same time there was an undefined feeling unlike anything Lily had ever felt before. Violetta appeared not as a smiling figure, but as an emotional representation of love, a love held in the purest form. Lily stood for several minutes holding on to that moment, until a flame in the center of the room burst upward extravagantly, erupting the silence between them. And even though Violetta had stopped smiling, Lily felt as though the love had dispersed into her being, the atmosphere, and everything around them. The love still existed, it was just hidden from plain sight.

"How do I heal?" Lily asked, although she felt conflicted, for the memories of what she was healing from confused her. "I don't even know what I need to heal from ..."

"Then that is where you must begin," Violetta replied, walking toward Lily. "The first step to heal is through acknowledging what has been done."

"How do I know what has been done though? I don't know if Jade has died. I am yet to find the pieces."

"Why are you looking down here then?" Violetta asked as her eyes lowered sincerely. And rightly so: what was Lily doing here, seeking answers from another, when all Violetta was doing was telling her that she held the answers herself? "Yes exactly. You are looking for a healer, forgetting you are your own greatest one," Violetta replied, as though reading Lily's mind.

"I guess I wanted to ask you if it was true that she had died?"

As Lily thought of Queen Jade's passing she saw a blurry image of Jade wandering amongst the flames below with a trail of dark smoke floating behind her.

"No one ever dies, you know that."

"Is it also true that a merman killed her?" Lily asked, wondering if the merman spoken about was Indigo.

"We all believe what we want to believe."

"So, it is true?" Lily stated, although she knew that Violetta would probably not confirm it to her.

Violetta looked back at Lily: no response, as expected. The tips of her eyelashes grew up high past her eyebrows, and the fine points took diamonds from her face and fluttered them down to the ground. "How can I find out?"

"How does anyone find out the truth? By confronting it," Violetta replied sternly this time and Lily felt a little bit silly for not knowing the obvious answer. She was cowering like a little girl, allowing the fear of what was to take over rationality of her mind.

"I'm too scared," Lily replied, bowing her head low; the idea of returning to the land of Tehar terrified Lily. She felt ashamed of her response too. Where was the girl who believed that she was guided and supported? She knew she could be brave, but when the time came to be challenged, she was willing to walk backward into a world of fear.

"There is nothing to be feared from what has already passed you. It's already happened. But the problem arises when you hold on to that energy. It was an experience that you felt and need to honor so that it can be let go. We heal through acknowledging, forgiving, and releasing," Violetta explained, delivering the words with no emotion. "Take a step to the left," she continued.

As Lily did so, a duplicate version of herself was revealed. And it stood there, as a mannequin. Completely still and quiet. Lily felt as though she was looking at herself for the first time. It wasn't the same as a mirror, or a photograph. She was a different person.

"I'm going to show you what I can see," Violetta said as she placed her hands above Lily's body.

Lily's body began to shake lightly as an outer bubble of white-and-violet light circled outside of her.

"This is your aura and it's always pure and innocent, unless you have trapped energy. Unless you are choosing to hold on to the pain, then this energy will remain stagnant," Violetta continued, as she hovered her hands over Lily's stomach, revealing a thick knot of brown light. As Violetta displayed the energy Lily could feel the knot in her stomach tighten. Like a heavyweight of stones weighing her down.

"It's sitting here, in your solar plexus chakra. Your confidence is shaken, your power is slightly off balance. You feel as though you don't know what to do." Violetta placed her hand over the top of Lily's brow where a dark swirl of black light twirled in a vortex. "And it's here as well, on your third eye chakra. Your intuition is thrown off. You followed your intuition before, but now you are scared. You aren't sure if it is the right way. Because it led you to pain."

Lily felt her head weigh heavy as Violetta revealed thoughts in her mind that she didn't know existed. Yes, she felt as though she was carrying a heavyweight around in her body. As though the pain of times past was a recurring problem that never disappeared, it was just waiting for the right opportunity to resurface. And it was true, she hated her intuition sometimes; she used to listen to it but how could she when it led her to pain? She hurt others and herself from her actions, and it was all from listening to her intuition.

"You need to heal and let this energy go so that something new can breathe in its space. Until you let go of it, nothing new will enter your life."

"Everything you say is correct, Violetta. There's just one thing that haunts me. Why did my intuition lead me to such a tragedy?"

"It happened the way it was meant to. Life is full of pain and love. They need each other to exist, and yet, they don't exist at all," Violetta replied, blinking slowly. Everything around Lily had slowed down now, even the flame flickered in soft motions.

"How do I fix this?" Lily pleaded as the words exited her mouth as slowly as the movements around.

"Don't you realize it yet? This world is your creation. It's a reflection of the internal world going on inside of you. How can there be peace if you aren't at peace with yourself? With what you've done?"

"How do I forgive myself if Jade is dead because of me? I don't deserve my forgiveness."

Violetta looked to Lily with no sympathy, no judgement either. Just a moment of listening. Violetta was holding space for Lily to figure this out on her own. And together the two stared at each other. Lily looked at the incredibly powerful empress in front of her. The feeling of her power was daunting to the young girl. She felt an immediate sense of respect, and willingness to obey her every command. Lily wished that she too held that same confidence. Lily took a deep breath and allowed the silence to provide her with the clarity she needed.

"I do deserve forgiveness," Lily rectified, holding her head a little higher. "I need to visit Tehar."

"Are you ready to return?"

"But what about the war?"

"Lily, this war existed for many years before you arrived here, and it will continue to exist for many years after. It is not for you to help, they need to help themselves."

"No matter what happens? No matter what change I do?" Lily begged for a different answer, she felt defeated before she had even taken her first steps toward change.

"Somewhere, someone will be feeling this anger and hate. It's not up to you to change that, it's just a necessary part of life."

"Why though? Why must there be hate? And evil? And anger?"

"Because everyone is in different stages of growing and evolving. Everyone is in different stages of loving themselves. And we will never all be caught up to the point of equality. We need to go through these emotions to get to the other side. Hate is a pathway to love. And once you arrive to love, you will never turn back."

Lily frowned at Violetta trying to understand what she was saying. She knew the powerful Empress shared great wisdom in her words, but to dismiss the need to help another and only focus on herself felt selfish, and the opposite of what Lily believed in.

"Are you ready to return?" she asked again, as though signaling their time together was finished.

"Yes." Lily nodded as the duplicate version of herself disappeared. "But wait, where are my friends? Why can't I find Karisma or Jacques on the land of Otor? Why does everything look so different now" Lily asked as she recalled Karisma's treehouse with the broken cups and bizarre emptiness.

"Because you are not the same person who you were before." Violetta replied, moving closer to Lily. "As you evolve and grow your life path sometimes separates from those you love. But their energy and wisdom will always be with you even though you aren't walking alongside each another."

"But I don't want our paths to separate. I loved Karisma like a mother, and Jacques was so jolly." Lily said as she smiled, remembering their positive energy. Karisma's kindness was a feeling that stayed with Lily long after her visit. The way she selflessly cared for Lily based purely on a desire to share her own happiness. It was an experience that had opened Lily's eyes to a different way of life and she cherished it fondly.

"Then remember them like that."

Lily nodded solemnly.

"Will I ever see them again?" Lily asked, feeling a pinch of sadness weigh heavy in her heart.

"They will appear on your journey when you need them the most. Come now, it's time for you to return." Violetta replied as she created the ball again as before, taking each of the elements from around her, suffocating them into the space between her hands.

She blew gently on the ball full of fire, water, and dirt, and upon doing so it grew bigger, and bigger. When it was larger than herself, she blew it toward Lily. As the bubble touched Lily's body it molded into her, and she was no longer standing on the rock, but instead, inside the bubble, now floating above Violetta. She floated up high above the fire, through the water, and along the space full of dirt. The dirt turned into a tunnel, and before she knew it she was right back where she started, standing in the middle of the cave, looking back over the fire that hovered to the underworld.

Lily sat on the edge of the mountain cliffs for several minutes as she reflected over her conversations with Violetta. She finally felt an understanding as to why she had come to Sa Neo again, but with the words of Violetta telling her to heal, she wondered how it referred to her life. But as she reflected she realized, if she was being completely honest with herself, she probably never did "heal" properly after her last visit to Sa Neo. She had left ashamed, responsible, and with regret, even though she learned that she needed to let go and move on. She was forced to let go of the past by leaving the magical world, but did she ever truly let go? Probably not. And here it was, haunting her in her dreams until she faced her reality.

She knew that she needed to know the truth about what happened to Jade, and whether her friend Silvia had ever escaped. But Lily was terrified to return to Tehar just now. Still, something stirred within Lily greater than her own need for healing. It was the desire to help another, despite her heart crying over the spilled blood that could have been the result from her past mistakes. And so she did what was necessary, she pulled out the green crystal stone and closed her eyes.

eleven

Tehar and Mia Veol

Lily arrived on the land of Tehar, and stood upon the green crystal-pebbled beach. She looked down at her feet, and all the memories of looking at those green pebbles so many times before flashed back through her mind. She felt strange. All the hairs on the back of her neck pricked up tall, and a shiver took over her body. She felt as though she could feel Jade's energy, her presence still near her. She looked around quickly to be sure. But there was no one there. Lily looked at the palm trees that lined the shoreline along the beach; they felt heavy with too much heat. The climate had continued to change after she had left, for the temperature on Tehar used to be quite delightful, but now it felt like that of a humid heatwave. Regardless, Lily continued to walk along the shoreline, interested to see what had become of Queen Jade's castle. But as she walked closer, she could see the same sign that once lay before—with a big "Queen Jade's Castle." Lily stopped in her footsteps. *Was it true or not?* she wondered. She didn't want to see Jade, but who was ruling this land? And why would they keep the castle still there?

Lily wasn't ready to find out. She knew that she needed to confront her deepest fear and regret, but now was not the time. She couldn't handle it. So she walked in the opposite direction, toward the marketplace that she once went to with Silvia. But before she made it there, she stumbled upon a village. It was a place that Lily had actually never been to before, despite her time spent in Tehar. She walked along the green crystal pathway and stared at the houses around her. The village was quite elaborate in contrast to any other villages that she had seen on the other lands. The architecture of each house was completely unique, with their own flamboyant style. One had a large front yard, full of perfectly cut green grass, but a very tiny house, and along the perimeter of the garden was a tall bush of green roses.

Across from this house with a fence of roses sat a peculiar house in the shape of a round bowl, almost like a sphere. The edge of it was made from a copper-looking metal. There were no doors, no windows, but a giant circle roof that was cut out. It looked very futuristic. Next to the sphere house was a Japanese-inspired space with a large pagoda, and a back fence full of bamboo trees and a lovely Zen garden in the front. This space had miniature bonsai trees and small white pebbles and it looked very inviting. The sound of trickling water could be heard from the street and Lily wondered if there was a fountain behind the house perhaps. She stood on the edge of the fence to get a better look when she felt a small tap on her shoulder. When Lily turned around there was a small elf standing before her wearing a pale green one piece suit and a matching top hat.

"Hello there!" The elf said with a wide smile that stretched across from ear to ear. "Come with me please." he continued, waving his hand and walking along the path.

He turned his head every now and again to check that Lily was following and finally stopped at a wooden stand with a painted sign above that said—Hugs For You.

But before Lily could reply the little elf had wrapped his tiny arms around one of Lily's legs and the two stood there for several seconds as she felt a rush of energy shoot up through her leg and into her body.

"Did you feel my boost of loving energy?" The elf asked raising his eyebrows as he let go.

"Yes, oh, thank you." Lily replied as she nodded, still buzzing from the vibrations the elf had shared.

"With pleasure!"

And with that, the elf jumped up onto the windowsill and sat on the edge, waiting for the next person who wanted a hug to walk by.

"Do you stand here all day giving hugs?"

"Pretty much." He nodded. "You never know when one little hug could save someone's life!"

"That's very true, my world could use more people like you in it." Lily replied, smiling at the elf's devotion. "And so, do you spend all day here just waiting for people?"

"No, love, this is where I live. Look down here." the elf said as he jumped over the other side of the window.

Lily peeked her head through and stared at a small opening that led to a large downstairs bedroom.

"I like living underground here, if the heat gets too much it's nice and cool and so peaceful!" The elf smiled as he jumped onto his bed like a child proudly displaying his space.

"It really does look lovely!" Lily said as she examined the room closely.

She adored the layout and cosiness of it. And more so, she just loved the elf's admiration of his own space. She hoped that one day her future house would give off the same excitement.

"What else can I help you with miss?" the elf asked as he jumped back up through the window to join Lily. "I haven't seen you around here before. Although we do get a lot of visitors this time of year."

"Oh really, and what kind of things do they look at?"

"Oh you know, the usual. Our markets here in Tehar are the grandest in all of the world!"

"Ah yes," Lily replied, remembering the lovely time she had there, meeting the yellow eyed man, and the box of scrolls she was gifted.

"But do you want to know the biggest attraction of this land?" The elf moved closer to Lily, tipping the top of his hat up to look her in the eyes.

"Please, do tell me."

"Well, come close." the elf whispered, as he encouraged Lily to move her ear near him. "Everyone comes to see the Queen who rose from slavery!"

"They do?" Lily's eyes opened wide as she leaned closer to the elf.

"Yes! They do." the elf replied. "There's a fantastic story about a foreign girl from another universe who visited Sa Neo and set her free!" The elf's eyes twinkled as he told the story, and he patted on the edge of his jacket, straightening out the fabric.

Lily felt strange as the elf talked about the story. *A foreign girl, setting someone free. It couldn't be Mia Veol,* she wondered? Lily often thought about Mia Veol too and whether she ever did set herself free.

"What's the Queen's name?"

"Mia Veol." The elf replied proudly. "Oh, she has a heart of pure beauty that Queen. You must go visit her!"

Lily blinked her eyes three times to make sure she wasn't dreaming. She couldn't believe it! Did she really help Mia Veol to escape? A smile from the center of Lily's heart floated up through her throat and she sighed with a great relief, knowing that finally one good thing that had come from her last visit to Sa Neo.

"Yes, yes please. How do I find her?"

"Head to the wooden pole in the middle of the road there, and then follow the signs. You can't miss it! You simply can't!" The elf replied as he jumped down and pointed with a long stick to the center of the village.

"Thank you so much! Have a lovely day, and thank you for the hug!" Lily replied as she waved the elf goodbye and walked in the direction he suggested.

She continued along the path full of unusual houses until she reached a long wooden pole in the middle of the road with almost 30 signs hammered to it. The signs had so many wonderful things written on them. There was reiki, crystal healing, and chakra realigning, and then at the very bottom of the tall piece of wood was a great sign that read "Queen Mia Veol."

A small butterfly was waiting on top of the wooden pole, and as soon as Lily tapped on Mia Veol's sign, the butterfly leapt up into the air and flew through the village. Lily quickly hurried after it, not letting it out of her sight. It wove through the streets, and through many houses, until it reached one in particular.

In front of Lily now stood a short bridge that crossed over a lake which led to a beautiful wooden arch entrance. On top of the archway lay pink roses and the words "Mia Veol." As Lily walked over the bridge, she could see colorful fish swimming below and little green frogs jumping around. Lily reached the other side of the bridge where a large door now appeared in front of her. But the door was not connected to a house. It was an empty door that floated as though in midair. And if Lily peered behind it, she would see purely the reflection of herself, as though it were a mirror. Lily lifted up her hand to knock, but before she could, the door opened on itself, revealing the entry to an enormous house.

"Hello ..." Lily called out as she poked her head through the door. But the interior of the house was quite unexpected. For even though she had walked through the dense forest, she was now looking through a floor-to-ceiling window that overlooked a great mountain range. The tips of the mountains were frosted with different decorations, some with snow, some with thick green grass, some with a field of flowers, and some were a great desert rock. It was a combination of all different mountains but in one picture. Lily was drawn to it, and she walked closer to the imagery, mesmerized.

She reached the glass window, and as she placed her hand on it, the scene changed once more; this time, it turned into her backyard. A strange uncanny feeling washed over Lily, as she stared at the familiar view she used to look at every day from her veranda.

"Is it really you?" came a voice from behind as the scenic view changed back to the mountain range.

Lily turned around. In front of her stood a beautiful tall and slender young girl, only a few years older than Lily's own age. Her hair was a soft strawberry blonde, and it was combed loosely around her head. Her eyes were a deep green, very similar to Lily's, with great depth. She wore a pale-green silk dress that hugged her body loosely. And on top of her head sat a flower crown, with magnificent flowers of all shapes and sizes and colors.

"You remember me?" Lily asked, nervously.

"Of course." Mia smiled as she walked closer to Lily, holding her gaze. "It's because of you that I am free." She opened her hands in a symbolic gesture of liberation, and as she did so, Lily felt lighter. It was as though Mia was handing Lily a gift of gratitude. "May I?" she asked, opening her arms to hug Lily.

Lily nodded shyly, opening her arms to embrace Mia. As their bodies touched Lily recalled their encounter vividly. Mia Veol as a trapped butterfly, beautiful and held under an enchanted spell. It brought tears to Lily's eyes, knowing that she had done something good in her life, and helped another. The two giggled as they let go, and Mia held Lily's hands, smiling with love.

"And, I hear you're the Queen here now?" Lily asked, recalling the excitement on the elf's face as he delivered her the news.

"They call me that, but I wish to be treated the same way. I am merely here to ensure that the village is looked after always."

Lily smiled with relief; *what a beautiful leader to only want the best for people,* she thought. *Such a selfless act. If only more people acted this way.*

"And so this means that Jade *is* dead! But why keep her castle? I don't understand why you wouldn't knock it down?" Lily asked, puzzled. It only felt right to destroy the exact prison that once held her hostage.

Mia frowned strangely and she bit the corner of her lip, unsure of how to explain.

"Jade still lives in Tehar."

As Mia uttered the words that Lily feared to be true, a sense of terror overtook Lily's body. She felt as though she couldn't breathe. She was overwhelmed with fearful thoughts, and they circled around in her head like a tornado, flickering in her eyes, and swirling in her mind. Her breathing started to get heavy, as though just the mere mention of her name would bring her near. And that the thought of her being called upon would somehow trap Lily into the land forever.

"Lily, are you okay?" Mia soothed, as she sat Lily onto the closest sofa. "You look pale."

"It can't be, it just can't be," Lily said as she shook her head in her hands. "I thought that Jade had died?" Lily felt terrible as she wished death upon another. But it wasn't as simple as that. The torture that Jade had commanded as a dictator was worse than Lily had ever experienced. Jade was the result of true evil.

"She did pass on from this life." Mia bowed her head in respect. "But her spirit is caught in the Middle World, and she still floats amongst the castle. She has not let go."

Lily looked to Mia, horrified. The feeling of a ghostly Queen haunting the lands felt almost worse than Jade's actual existence in Sa Neo.

"But, why?" Lily said as she looked down and swallowed hard, feeling more confusion overflow in her head.

"It's believed that if a spirit has not passed on to the upper world, it's because someone here has not let her go."

Mia sat down next to Lily on the soft green sofa. And with her lovely delicate hand she stroked Lily's arm, as though she was soothing Lily as much as herself.

"Who do you think has not let her go?"

"Rumors are circulating that it's perhaps the result of Queen Allura, on the land of Praza, do you know her?"

"Unfortunately." Lily replied as she rolled her eyes, cringing at the idea of such a horrid person.

It was strange, Lily didn't think there could be someone who was worse than Jade, but Allura didn't just act evil, she made a point to ruin the lives of others purely for her own pleasure—she was monstrous.

"Allura and Jade were twin sisters."

"What?" Lily gasped in a great rush of air and she held it for several seconds before remembering to let it go. "Twins?" she finally said, breathing out noisily.

"Yes. They entered this world together as conjoined twins, connected as one by their arms," Mia said as she stood up from the chair. "But when they arrived, a lightning struck down between them, slicing them in half. And the great movement of such a miracle pushed them to opposite sides of the world." Mia paused, allowing the image of what that must have felt like to slice through the space. "But there was one rule. The great heavens above told them that if they were to ever meet, they would be joined back together. The desire of their Souls wanting to be as one."

Lily's eyes open widely as she hung on to Mia's words, trying to understand the emotion that she was feeling. Could she actually be feeling sorry for the sisters? *How terrible to be separated from your loved one*, she thought. And for a moment, it kind of made sense. The harshness of their actions, their inability to feel complete. Their desires to always attack another, or feed off their power, in order to stabilize their own existence.

"And so, they never saw each other again?" Lily asked, feeling faint-hearted, as she imagined the thought of never seeing her father again.

"Never," Mia replied, looking out through the great landscape window. "Whether they entered this world to experience their life separated or joined together was never known. But the truth is, they were born leaders. If they were to live together, who would lead? And so, they swore to never see each other again."

Lily stood up to join Mia near the glass window. The landscape had now changed again to the outside forest, and they stood in front of a field full of wild horses.

"But now that Jade has passed, Allura can finally see her. It's believed that she travels when the moons are the fullest from the magic of the mermaid's tail."

Lily recalled the ceremony with Allura. And how after she ate and drank, she had seemed to attract a deeper layer of consciousness. She remembered that when she looked at the Queen her body lay lifelessly on the ground.

"Can Jade come back to Sa Neo?"

"The energy of her spirit still lives here. There are two parts to her Soul. The exterior that we see, her ghost, roams through here in our reality, but the truth is, she is walking in the Middle World. The doorway to creation is the same portal to exit. And for Jade to move on, and recreate into another entity, she needs to leave. But she can't, she's trapped. And so are the evil thoughts of her energy, echoing throughout this world."

Lily took a deep breath as she stared out to the landscape next to Mia Veol. She felt as though the more she wandered through Sa Neo, the more complex and twisted it had become. There was evil trapped in shadows, haunting memories of the past, not letting go. Her mind was overflowing with thoughts. She already felt overwhelmed to help the revolution, but now it seemed there was an even bigger problem to deal with.

"Are you okay, Lily?" Mia asked, starting to walk Lily back to the safeness of the sofa once more.

But Lily was too upset, and so she confessed everything. The truth about her regretful exit from this world, the dreams, and callings that she had to return. The disappointment in Indigo's face when he saw her. The terror of genocide in the land of Praza. The slaughtering of animals for one's own pleasure. And now she had learned about Jade, roaming the world and haunting all to come. How could she heal this world now? Lily wanted to give up. It sounded impossible. It felt impossible.

"I'm so silly believing that I could do this. This mess is just too big," Lily argued out loud. "I'm just a small girl, I'm no match to take on the power of a Queen! I'm a fool to have returned."

Lily could feel the edges of her cheeks begin to burn as small bumps of blood pulsated up to the surface of her skin, creating an enflamed red patchiness on her face. The feelings of being worthless began to creep back up into her mind, and she sobbed silently, forgetting that she was in another's company. Forgetting that she had traveled so far, all she could feel was that she had accomplished nothing, for she was right back where she started.

"Lily, you're more magical than you know," Mia soothed with her soft, loving voice. "There are powers within you, I can see them and feel them. Look."

Mia held her hands over the front of Lily's hands, and as she did so, electrical bolts of lightning erupted in the sky above. The backdrop of the glass window had changed again to resemble Lily's backyard, and right in front of their eyes, the electrical bolt of lightning had fastened to the ground, the exact same way it had done back home, before she first began her journey.

"What do you see, Lily?" Mia asked, as she turned to look at the window with Lily.

"It's my backyard at home. There's lightning," Lily said as the first thoughts of her father came into her mind. And how long she really had traveled for this time. "I've seen this before."

"But it's only happening now," Mia replied, but as she looked to Lily her eyes told another story. A story that suggested that there were two worlds co-existing at the same time. For how was it possible that the lightning bolt struck in both places, and Lily was viewing it at the exact same place, at the exact same time.

"This is your home," Mia spoke again, pointing to the view of the backyard. "This is where your strength was born. And that lightning, that's the energy that created you. Your power, your true essence of being. The divine lies within you, she is sleeping. We need to wake her up."

Mia's voice spoke with such beauty, it reminded Lily of a sweet lullaby she used to sing when she was younger. The way the tones of her voice would lift with soothing words of admiration. And with a single tear, Lily wept. An overload of emotion once more. Still, she felt as though this task was too big, that she was too small, and that this world didn't care about her, not really. But even so, she felt lost within herself. The confidence to be true to who she was. She desperately wanted to awaken the divine within her.

"How do I do it?"

"You have both masculine and feminine aspects within you, and both are needed to take on this challenge to lead the people. The masculine energy supports your ambition, your ability to accomplish this goal and stay focused. But the feminine is of equal importance, it is through this that your body and Soul are nourished. Your masculine wouldn't survive without the feminine, and the same way, the feminine would have no direction or purpose without the masculine energy. Both are needed to fulfill the true destiny of your life," Mia explained using her hands to create a vision to accompany her words.

"And how do you know the Divine within me is sleeping?" Lily asked, although she knew that it was true. For there was something within her that was stopping her from moving forward. Lack of confidence was one thing, but the desire to change did not exist either.

"Because you are questioning your purpose here. From the stories you tell me, you have been granted the signs along the path to move forward, this is what you need to do. And yet, I can feel that your heart energy is blocked."

Mia held her hand near Lily's heart. And as she did so, Lily felt a painful twisting knot, exactly as Mia had described. The feeling of heartache was unlike a pressure point, but the emotional outburst of seeing the truth and unable to take the steps forward to play this role out. Lily believed that there was Divine spirit energy inside of her, and yet the confidence to awaken it, and let it live true was impossibly beyond reach.

"You can feel it, can't you, Lily?"

"Yes," Lily replied as her eyes closed in anguish.

"Let me heal your heart," Mia said, as she stood up. "Lie down there on the sofa."

Lily lay down on the heavenly plush sofa. The edges of the green fabric felt like a soft layer of moss found only in the most luscious of rainforests. And from just the care of another person saying let me heal you, Lily already felt like a part of her was healed. She molded her body into the sofa as though it were the grass on the ground, and as though Mother Nature was nourishing her heart. And perhaps that was a part of the process, this imagination that there was something from her exterior that could heal the interior. Lily closed her eyes and waited patiently for Mia's return.

But Lily fell asleep. And in her dreams she journeyed to a place far away. She was sitting up high, on top of the highest mountain she had ever seen before. But she could not see her body, only her eyes viewed the surroundings. And the world around her looked like neither her home, nor the world of Sa Neo. It was another sight, something even more incredible, if that was possible. It was a land full of green fields, and lush blue oceans, and flowers, and mountains, and an abundance of flora and fauna in every color imaginable. Lily stayed in her view, high up top, higher than anything she had ever seen before. She watched over the lands with pride, and strength. She felt a strong connection to the world around her, a sense of belonging, a feeling of contentment. She breathed in gently, looking at the view of something that would normally make her feel quite insignificant; instead, she felt as though this world was on view just for her. She was watching the incredible display of life around her, and it was glorious.

"Lily, we're finished," Mia cooed with her gentle voice, as she rubbed Lily's arm lightly. "How do you feel?"

Lily sat up refreshed and revitalized.

"I feel amazing, thank you," Lily replied, as she stretched her arms high above her head. She felt realigned somehow in her body. As though she had just completed a yoga course. She felt strength in her knowledge, and flexibility in her body. And the vision of what she had seen echoed through her mind.

"Where did you go?" Mia asked, a small mischievous smile as though she had traveled with Lily.

"In my dream, I felt as though I was on top of the world," Lily explained as she relived the memory once more. The deep breaths of clean air, and beautiful imagery of lush nature.

"How do you know it was a dream?" Mia said as she handed Lily a glass of refreshing water with crushed mint leaves.

"Do you think I actually went there?"

"Perhaps." Mia smiled as she, too, took a sip of water.

Lily drank hers too, slowly regaining consciousness, wondering where and how she traveled through her dreams, into her journey. "I can travel through my dreams?" Lily asked, unsure why the thought had never occurred to her before. "And if so, does that mean that I really did see Indigo those times? Or more importantly, does this mean I could find Jade in the Middle World? And release her?"

Lily wasn't even sure where these words had come from. The desire to travel to the Middle World was not something she had ever intended on doing, nor seeing Jade again. But now that her heart was realigned, and she felt the presence of both the masculine and feminine energies balanced within her body, the fear of what was no longer existed. The idea of releasing Jade felt like the most appropriate action; perhaps, she would be able to release the evil from the world at the same time too, she thought.

"There is one man who can help you travel to the Middle World. His name is King Devya of Deia and he is the great shaman of Sa Neo. He travels to the Underworld, the Middle World, and the Upper World. With him by your side, you will conquer any rite of passage."

"Then I shall go," Lily replied, standing up as she finished the glass of water. "Mia, I am so grateful for this visit."

"As am I," Mia replied as she stood up with Lily.

"Thank you for having faith in me.".

"It's not only me who has faith in you, it's the energy of the voices around you. Everyone in this world is supporting you. Never forget that," Mia replied, nodding kindly. "Our thoughts, although individual, are still a part of the unconscious collective, and together we push each other to create change."

"They are?" Lily asked, wondering how the world could be supporting her actions even though they didn't know.

"Yes, of course. The whole universe is behind you! Can't you feel it?" Mia said and she took hold of Lily's hands, encouraging her feel her way to the truth.

Lily quietened her mind and concentrated. She could feel a strange buzzing sensation through her body. Like tickles of excitement running through her veins. She finally felt as though she had a purpose, and even though she knew she didn't need a purpose to be happy, here she was, able to do something for someone else and that idea gave her the most satisfaction of all. She had an opportunity to make a difference in this world, the freedom to stand up for what she believed in. And by that one person moving forward, she could potentially help save thousands of others.

Lily smiled as she waved goodbye, feeling the strength of Mia by her side, and the world of Tehar. The land seemed to have aligned perfectly by itself with Mia now ruling it. And finally, Lily felt as though she had done something good. Something great was created in exchange for the heartache she had caused. As Lily walked back to the beach, she wondered if all greatness was balanced with heartache. Whether it was actually even possible to have complete positivity in the world at once. And with that thought, she pulled out the blue crystal from her pouch, cleared her mind, and tedimetaed to the land of Deia.

twelve

King Devya of Deia

Lily opened her eyes to the flat land of Deia. It looked exactly the same as she remembered it, open space of flat blue crystal rocks, with barely anything. No trees, no nature, just rock and air. Lily had visited it once before with Karisma, but this time she was not scared, and her voice did not shake. *I am stronger than I was before,* Lily thought to herself. She was older and wiser now.

Lily walked down the path in front of her, although it didn't appear to be much of a path, just thick flat rocks that added dimensions to her view. Lily felt clarity in her thoughts as she walked, and the voice in her heart was speaking clearly to her. In the far distance Lily could hear the sound of something beautiful. It started off as a subtle hint, a soft teardrop of noise, and as Lily closed her eyes to listen, she felt as though she heard the murmur of what a twinkling star might sound like. As Lily moved toward the sound she could finally see what it was. For there around her was a long free-hanging wind chime. The sheer volume of it was so powerful, Lily felt as though she could see the energy radiate off the instrument and fly up into the clouds. The faint breeze that moved through the land kissed the chimes and in turn they all kissed one another in a domino effect. It was mesmerizing to Lily. The whole land around her disappeared as she walked through the magnificent instrument. The sound and look of the chimes around her made her feel as though she was in another world. One that was full of sound vibrations that soothed and healed her body. She felt relaxed and energized at the same time. It was an enchanting combination of pure bliss.

Lily continued to walk between the gently moving chimes, and she whisked her hand along the instrument creating a new vibration. She felt as though she was a part of something raw and surreal. As she continued the pathway of chimes turned into a circle, and in the center sat a man in deep meditation. Lily stopped in her footsteps, not wanting to disturb the man, but it was too late, he already sensed her energy.

"Welcome to the land of Deia," the man replied, opening his eyes and looking calmly at Lily.

His eyes were the same color as the crystals on the land, a soft blue. It reminded Lily of the color that could be seen in very shallow waters.

"Thank you," Lily replied with a calm smile. She was relaxed amongst the sound for the vibrations harmonized her core, and she felt completely at peace in his presence.

"I'm Devya," the man said as he stood up, revealing his strangely shaped clothes. They were thick fabrics of pale blue, and the edges were sharp, like a pointed iron. His outfit looked strangely futuristic, except for the thin plait of rope around his forehead, and his messy shoulder-length hair with bare feet.

"It's an honor to meet you, King Devya," Lily replied as she curtseyed lightly.

"The pleasure is all mine; please, just Devya is fine. Let me show you my land," the King said as he directed Lily through the chimes. They continued along the path until a vast space of emptiness lay out in front of them.

"This land doesn't have much nature anywhere, why is that?" Lily asked as she stared in awe at the brilliant backdrop of blue desert.

"Deia is the land of communication. There is too much electrical energy that transmutes here for wildlife to live."

"Electrical energy?" Lily asked as she looked up above, trying to see cords of electricity. But there was nothing but a bright blue sky.

"Yes, Lily, your voice emits a strong radiation of vibrational frequencies, it is here that everything channels to elsewhere. In the shortest moment you can possibly imagine, divide it into billions and that's how fast your communication can travel. Here, look," King Devya said as he pointed directly ahead. The sky around them grew dark, and tiny shooting bright lights shot through the air in long streams all around them. It moved above and below Lily, and even through her. Lily lifted her hand to cut through the beam of energy, but alas, the light hovered before and after, not stopping the cord.

"You see? This is why we must be mindful of our words, for they are absorbed even when we don't realize it."

Lily nodded. It made sense, yet she was surprised she had never thought about it before. She had a tendency to shy away from gossip at school or any kind of negativity. But she didn't know why.

King Devya waved his hand over his left shoulder, and the sky lit back up again. "It never gets dark here, the lights are too bright and shine all the time; it's impossible."

"So you can see and feel this communication, can you also hear it?"

"Yes, if I wished to. But it's a private connection shared between two people, I don't like to do it."

Lily thought about the power that Devya held of being able to tune into communication anywhere, and how magnificent that he didn't use that ability for his own personal gain. If someone were evil, they would abuse that power, but Devya was good-hearted. Lily realized that this was a perfect opportunity for her to find out if the land of Praza would support Allura's power being overthrown. For, despite Mia Veol's suggested support from the universe, the question still haunted Lily—was she standing out there all alone?

"Do you know about the war? Between the mermaids and Queen Allura?" Lily looked to Devya, curious to read his reaction. Whenever someone was told grave news Lily always watched their immediate facial and body language, it always spoke more to her than their words. Devya reacted as a normal ethical creature would have: a slight freeze in his stance, the acknowledgement that greed existed. There was no sign of watery tears in his eyes, he was strong, but Lily could see the compassion within him, it was as though his heart was beating outside his body, shooting love to those who were in pain. Yet Lily still felt outraged; how could so many leaders know of the slaughtering of innocents in the world and not do anything about it? How could they pass through their day?

"We have rules between lands. We cannot get involved. What happens on one land is unique to that land," Devya replied, sensing her displacement.

"But surely this is an exception to the rule?"

"It's not a matter of risking my life for others, I would gladly do it. But the truth is, it's impossible to wake up those who are choosing to sleep. So many of the people of Praza are voluntarily turning away from the truth. They are presented with honesty from all of us, but to admit they are wrong is to define their own stupidity, and I believe that they are too proud to give in." Devya nodded his head sadly.

"But we have to try, right? We have to believe that there is still good in the world. That corruption hasn't killed the spirit within? Would the people stand by me if I took this chance?"

Lily could see the faces of Marlina's children as she wished for change. It was those who were too tiny to do anything that she needed to help. And even though she had only just met the children a short time ago, it didn't matter. For those children represented fellow friends, they were family to her now.

"It is sad that such madness has occurred, I'm deeply sorry," Devya said as he crouched down to his knees. He put his hands in the blue crystal dirt and drew a circle four times. "Let us see the truth of the people, and what direction this war can go."

With one hand he gathered the small grains of crystals and walked over to one of the larger chimes which was almost a full arm's length wide. He sang a low-sounding vowel, and upon doing so, the chime shook, cracking through the center and revealing a low table made from charcoal. The table dipped low in the center, like a bowl, with sacred geometric patterns decorating the edge. The King tipped the crystal sand onto the charcoal table and as he did so, the blue grains moved through patterns on the plate.

"This war has been going on for many moons." Devya nodded, as the grains moved through positions as if foretelling a story in front of him. "The whole world, not including the Land of Praza, is against Queen Allura's ruling. But on the land of Praza, only half of the people will stand by you. And the other half are too fearful to go against the destiny of the land," Devya said as he rolled the small stones over onto each other, feeling their voice as he listened intently. "This war is the result of us not speaking our truth, for too many generations. For too many years we suppressed our voices, and now, we have lost what was ours. If we ignore the voice from our heart's calling, of our true desires, we will forget ourselves, and be swept into the crowd of another's dream." As Devya spoke the words of the stones, he used his hands to show the visual of communication blockages within his throat. Upon doing so, Lily felt a lump in her own throat and she swallowed profusely to try to clear it.

"The village folk of Praza have been told lies their whole life. The history was fabricated to suit Allura's needs. It's not right," Lily cried, devastated that someone could be so ethically corrupt for their own selfish needs.

Now everything became transparent. She could see how the corruption of one person's mind could poison the rivers of villages around it. And how the toxin from this unethical Soul had soiled the dirt for the next generations of people to come. Lily couldn't understand how people could be so idiotic. But then she took a step back and had a look at the situation from another light. Instead of pointing the blame she put herself into the eyes of those who stood by Allura. Perhaps they enjoyed playing the fool and living a life of ignorance. Thinking that nothing was happening and yet it was. Perhaps those who stood by Allura were receiving rewards in exchange for their silence.

"Devya, we need to show the world the truth about Allura. We need to tell them what really happened to Jade."

"Do you know what really happened?"

Lily looked back to Devya slightly stumped in her response.

"I feel so ashamed, Devya. I was so concerned about whether Jade was alive and what that meant for me that I forgot about everyone else." Lily bowed her head as she felt knots inside her stomach begin to turn. She felt sick. She thought she had come so far, wanting the best for others, but when the time came, she had forgotten about the truth of what she needed to do. She just thought selfishly about herself.

"Don't be so hard on yourself, Lily. Listen, you've realized what happened now, this is self-reflection. This is how you learn," Devya replied, smiling, and as he did so, the edges of his eyebrows curved slightly, lowering his braided headband around his face. "And you're putting yourself in the point of view of the people of Praza, that's self-awareness. You might feel like you are failing, but you really are just growing."

Lily nodded as Devya spoke, believing that she was absorbing his words, and she wanted to, she did. But she felt as though until she had something to truly show for her mistake, and until she had truly corrected this wrong, she couldn't be proud of herself. Nor of how far she had come.

"Devya, I came here seeking your help. It's believed that Jade is trapped in the Middle World. I want to help her pass over. It's my first step in hoping that Allura's evil may subside," Lily asked, remembering her true reason for visiting the land of Deia.

"It can be done, but not alone. We will need to go to the campground of the Apprentices; together we'll pull the great powers of the ancestors' primordial wisdom to assist you on this journey."

"Whatever it takes, I'm willing to do it." Lily took a deep breath as she vocalized her pact to the world. She would do everything she could to help bridge the gap of indifference. She believed that every creature deserved their space in the world, that they held the right to be who they wanted to be, and that they should live however they wished to live. She wasn't sure how she would help the others gain this knowledge, but she just knew that it had to be done. She was helping influence change. And even though every now and again her heart wavered, or her mind fluttered, and that hole in her chest that said she couldn't do it would sometimes scream louder than the other voices that said she could, she kept moving forward. Because there was no other way, other than forward.

thirteen

A Journey to the Middle World

Lily and King Devya walked together across the vast landscapes of empty skies, and blank canvases. The floor felt like a mirage the way it extended for miles; it was the same reflection of what was before, being repeated over and over again. At times, Lily grew weary, wanting water or food, but Devya instructed her that a fasting was necessary prior to the ceremony taking place.

After a long journey the two arrived at the campground of the Apprentices. It was a large campsite full of teepees set up in a grand circle, and in the center was a cushioned bed that seemed to rise above the ground just lightly, as though it was levitating. The bed was surrounded with wooden seats all around it, and a variety of musical instruments sat on the ground next to the seats. There were rattles and drums, large feather wands, and crystal and copper singing bowls. The Apprentices were already sitting on the seats, ready for Lily and Devya to arrive. On the edge of the circle sat four bonfires, and next to the side of the bonfire was a crystal altar with a variety of ingredients and instruments all over it. Upon Lily and Devya's arrival, the Apprentices all stood and bowed their heads lightly.

"Welcome," they chanted together in a long voice.

The Apprentices were dressed similar to Devya, except the colors of their skins were the most beautiful shades imaginable. They looked as though they were the descendants of indigenous tribes from different universes, for their eyes and faces changed shapes dramatically in comparison to one another. Their clothes were more minimal than King Devya's, and upon their skin they had painted sacred geometric artwork. Their appearance showed that they had great respect for themselves, their tribe, and where it was that they came from.

"These are the Apprentices," Devya said to Lily as he held his arm out. "They have all traveled many universes to come here and learn from one another. We are all as wise as each other, but we carry gifts from other worlds. They call themselves the 'Apprentices' because they are forever learning."

"Lovely to meet you all." Lily smiled as she was introduced. "Thank you for assisting us on this journey."

The Apprentices all nodded as they were spoken to. Even though no one replied to Lily, she had begun to understand that this was a land where words were unnecessary.

"Are you ready for this journey?" Devya asked Lily as he walked to the crystal altar.

The Apprentices followed and took their seats in a circle. Devya stood at the head of the circle by the altar and picked up a crystal bowl. Taking a piece of wood he tapped it against the bowl, creating a soft, harmonic vibration in the air. The Apprentices and Lily could all feel the sound move through their body, and an immediate stillness was present in the air, as though everything was just beginning and ending at once.

"I call upon spirit to aid Lily on this journey," Devya said, as he kissed the edge of the bowl and passed it to one of the Apprentices.

"I call upon spirit to aid Lily on this journey," chanted the next Apprentice as he too kissed the bowl and passed it onto the next, and the next one after that.

"You too, Lily," Devya instructed as Lily was asked to join in on the sacred ceremonial creation.

As Lily lifted the bowl to the edge of her lips an overflow of energy moved through her body. It was as though the bowl had captured a powerful concoction of strength, support, guidance, beauty, and grace, all in one motion. As though each spirit that moved within the Apprentice had blessed the bowl with the intention of helping Lily on her journey.

"The bark of silver's tongue," Devya said, as he picked up a wooden branch and peeled the piece of silver bark. "May the words flow with ease from your mouth, Lily, and enable you the change you wish to seek in the Middle World." Devya placed the bark on his forehead and passed the item around the circle.

The Apprentices followed the actions of Devya, and Lily too obeyed willingly. As each new item was added to the ceremony, a surplus of vibrating energy entered the space. When the ingredient had completed the circle Devya placed it inside the bowl.

"Spices of an open heart," Devya said as he ground the tiny seedlings of salted dust through his fingers, pouring it into a small container and onto the next person along. "May your heart guide you safely on this journey."

"The wings of the angelic ones," Devya said as he blew his breath onto the edges of the feather, allowing soft movements in the wings. "Travel with lightness and grace as you venture through the Middle World, and may you have a safe return." The wings fluttered in the air around the circle, moving past each of the Apprentices and Lily before making its way back to Devya and into the bowl.

"Now the last ingredient, the final piece that enables us swift travel between the worlds. The Soul of Sa Neo," King Devya said as he reached into the ground below, digging the crystals to the side. He continued to keep digging, pulling out blue crystals and placing them to the side, miraculously reaching down farther than possibly imaginable each time. And with his bare hands he pulled out a long strain of fire, the same color and vibration that Lily felt when she was with Violetta in the Underworld. The fire erupted with small bursts of energy from the ground, to which Devya placed the bowl upon.

"Thank you for blessing us with an abundance of energy, above and below," Devya recited, as he stretched his hand up high and twinkled his fingers. Upon doing so a stream of rain poured down in a long line, landing perfectly in the bowl. When satisfied with the amount he held his hands up against the edge of the bowl, and slowly, very slowly, the bowl rotated around on the fire, stirring the contents inside.

The Apprentices picked up their instruments and started to play altogether. Some were beating drums, shaking leaf rattles, and blowing through flutes. Each played in a harmonious tune, a long, drawn-out rhythm of perfectly pitched echoes.

"It's time," Devya said as he extinguished the fire, allowing the liquid in the bowl to harden into a thick, gooey syrup. "Come and lie down in the center, Lily." Devya motioned to Lily as they walked together to the levitating bed. "As you drink this sacred drink, I want you to set your intention for this journey to the outer worlds. Do you remember why you came?"

Lily nodded her head in reply. "To walk with Jade and take her to the upper world." Lily didn't even know where the words had come from, nor how she would even know how to walk with her up there. But the question of how did not even seep through Lily's thoughts; she had a strange understanding of knowing.

"All stand as I ignite the commencement of this ceremony," Devya said as he walked around the circle slowly, blowing a long trail of sweetgrass smoke across everyone. When he reached Lily, he blew the smoke from the very top of her forehead down to her feet and back up around.

Devya pulled out a flute and turned his body to his right side. He whistled through the flute in a soft-sounding rhythm and began to speak outward toward the energetic fields.

"To the winds of the South, I call upon the Great Serpent. Guide us to shed the layers of ourselves that do not serve our journey."

Devya half swallowed some water that was in a small bottle and spat it out into the air as the sentence was finished. The liquid splashed through the air and up high, twisting in colors of different shades. He then turned a quarter around and spoke again.

"To the winds of the West, I call upon dear Sister Jaguar. Protect us on this journey as we move through our dreams past the material world. Provide us with the strength of warrior spirit to combat all that disrupts our peace." And once again, Devya spat the liquid in his bottle up high, holding the flaming sweet grass in his opposite hand as he talked.

"To the winds of the North, I call upon the Royal Hummingbird. To the Souls who fly with our great ancestors and with our great ancient ones. Whisper your wisdom through the air, and share your vision with us, so that we may create a better world."

He turned once more, spitting the liquid and blazing the smoke through the space.

"To the winds of the East, I call upon the Great Eagle. Fly through the sky and show us how to bring our vision into light. Together we will embark on new territories, through the domain of manifestation and enlightenment."

As he turned the last time, Lily could feel the energy around her rise up high. It was as though each wind that blew from the corner of the direction that Devya had spoken to was listening, and the air joined into the circle, twirling around like a tornado. The energy around Lily felt incredibly strong, almost turbulent like. It was overpowering, intoxicating, and yet inviting all at once.

Devya placed the sweetgrass and water jar on the ground and picked up a copper-ended wooden wand that was engraved. The edges of the wand held thick crystals, and the center was painted with copper slithers that looked like lightning had erupted from the inside out. With the edge of the wand he scooped up a portion of the syrup from the bowl.

"With this plant medicine, I bless thee, and I invite you to walk amongst the spirits," Devya recited as he spoon fed the syrup into Lily's mouth.

The taste of the syrup was revoltingly bitter. It was a sharp flavor that felt as though it burned her tongue as it slowly moved down her throat and into the pit of her stomach. The energy of the syrup continued to move inside of her, splashing like wild currents out in the far sea. She closed her eyes and lay down, allowing the plant medicine to take control.

"I will follow you, wait for me there ..." were the last words that Lily heard in her mind from Devya.

Lily had entered a deep meditative trance within seconds. The beating of her heart had slowed down and was now purring in alignment with the sound of the drums around her. Her breath flowed as though it were a long stream of air that moved as one with the universe. With every deep inhale she took a piece of the atmosphere inside of her, and as she exhaled, she gave the gift back, as it wafted through the lands, regenerating itself with the trees and water. Slowly, breath by breath, she relaxed further, allowing the sounds of the music to take her through a journey into the afterlife of outer worlds.

Lily opened her eyes to see a white owl flying over her. She stood up and held her arm out, allowing the owl to perch upon her arm. Devya was still standing next to her, along with the other Apprentices around the circle. But now, they all held a glowing light in a diamond shape around them. The light split through the ground, pointing down below and up high. Everyone was still in ceremony, playing their musical instruments and chanting. Lily patted the feathers of the owl on her arm and turned back around to the levitating bed. It was here that she could see her own body. She was peering over the stillness of herself, slowly breathing in and out, her heart beating in line with the rhythm. She had left her body in the world of Sa Neo as she journeyed through as a spiritual Soul. But instead of feeling nervous or scared, Lily was completely calm. She was relaxed, with no emotion. The thought of her as a separate entity was explained to her many times, especially through her journey in Sa Neo, but this was the first time that Lily could actually feel and see it, and finally, it actually seemed to make sense. She could understand the unique gift of her Soul choosing her own body. When "she" entered the world, she chose to be Lily. Every day that "she" woke up, she chose to live her life in Lily's body, and there was something very surreal and magical about that decision. Her journey was not by chance, it was a well-planned experience, and the depth of that truth was almost too powerful to completely comprehend.

The owl leapt from Lily's arm and flew up high above, hovering once more. Lily looked up and watched as the owl disappeared from her sight. It didn't fly away, it just wasn't there anymore. At the same time the atmosphere around Lily changed, absorbing all light from her view. The sound of the music had ceased too, and the Apprentices, and King Devya. She was standing all alone, in the Middle World.

"Where do I go?" Lily asked out loud as the sound of her voice echoed like thunder through the dark world around her.

A small ball of fire rolled past her. It moved gracefully at first, and then with force, from one direction behind to in front of where she stood. The sound of a soft whisper moved through the air into her ears and it whispered, "Honor the light."

Lily walked in the direction of where the fire balls rolled past her. As the flame of light came closer, Lily could see the world around her light up for a split second. But it was terrifying, and Lily wished that it remained dark. For around her were hundreds of floating spirits, mourning, screaming and pleading for mercy. They were wandering aimlessly so close to where Lily walked, but could only be seen while the balls of flames rolled past her, for when they did not, the world was dark, and Lily couldn't see anything at all.

"I'm here," came a familiar voice next to Lily.

She looked to her right and there stood King Devya, holding a tall wand of flaming light. Lily tried to smile with gratitude, but the denseness in the air around her prevented her from expressing any emotion. It was as though the feeling of happiness had been sucked out of her.

"Thank you for coming," she replied, somberly.

Devya nodded at Lily and together they walked through the space of floating entities. But now the fire from the wooden wand that Devya held lit up the whole land, and Lily could see the faces of the entities that walked by their side. An elderly lady was crouched on the ground, crying into her hands. And another, a small boy of five, was holding a ball and throwing it at the ghostly figures while running around screaming. The sounds of sorrow pierced through the land, and an overwhelming sense of misery and grief was present. Lily felt an unbearable sadness take over her mind, and she felt a strong urge to cry. Lily kneeled down and surrendered to the pain, allowing the tears to move through her. They fell hard onto the ground but when they touched the surface they lifted back up, bouncing like little balls, and flying up into the sky as though the tears never fell at all.

"Stand up, Lily. Protect your energy, you are taking on their pain body! It's not yours to take. Let the energy flow around you, don't absorb it."

Lily could hear the words of Devya and she wanted to obey him, she really did, but the power of emotion was taking over her sense of rationality. And so in between muffled breaths of deep inhalation, she cried. Lily felt as though the sky was weighing heavily on her head, forcing her to look down and flushing tears through her eyes in a desperate need to be released. Slowly, very slowly, the feeling of small, itching feet began to crawl over her. The feeling was so slow and almost therapeutic; she didn't notice it at first. But before she could blink, her entire body was covered in a swarm of ants. They were feeding upon her tears. The tiny ants crawled up her neck, into her ears and right next to her eyes, feasting the fresh tears that flowed out. She couldn't move.

"HELP ME, DEVYA!" Lily screamed as the ants began to crawl into her mouth. Her emotion of sorrow quickly began to change to anger, as she felt hopelessly stuck in her circumstances.

The evil entities that surrounded them began to circle Lily, and they hovered closely, staring and laughing.

Devya pulled a piece of white sage from his cloak and he banged the bottom of the flaming wand to the ground and pointed it above them.

"I call upon the energy of Gaia. Bring forth the light that lies within all of us, show us the way forward," Devya said as he lit the edge of the white sage and proceeded to blow smoke over Lily. As soon as the smoke enveloped Lily's body, the ants began to crawl away. They scurried off her skin quickly and onto the ground, disappearing into nothing.

"We must move quickly, do as I say," Devya said, as he continued to blow the smoke around Lily. "Hold your arms out wide, and circle them around and then over your head."

Lily did as she was told, and the smoke circulated quickly, finally settling in the shape of a sphere around her body.

"You are cleansing your energy field and creating a protection around it, so that nothing can harm you. Repeat after me: 'I demand my sacred space.'"

"I demand my sacred space," Lily recited, as the smoke began to clear, and a white light took over in its place.

"Again, and louder!" Devya said, knocking the wooden wand against the ground again; it shuddered in echoes through the land.

"I DEMAND MY SACRED SPACE," Lily recited again, feeling stronger than before, and she stood proudly envisioning the light bubble of energy protecting her in a sphere.

"Good, no harm will come. Let's find Jade." Devya nodded as he moved forward.

The lost spirits that hovered in the atmosphere now parted as Lily walked through the land. Their cries of grief and anger were still present, but now, Lily had no connection with them, no contact, no emotional empathy. It was as though they didn't exist at all. Together, Devya and Lily walked through the Middle World. Now that Lily had created the bubble of protection around her energy field, she could see the land in a different light. Yes, she was still surrounded with devilish entities, but in between these were the strength of the trees, the rocks, and the mountains. Each creation of nature was alive and pulsating with spirit. She could see the energy reach high above the physical object on the land, and it played up above, as though it had chosen to enter that space of creation at that exact moment in time.

In the distance, Lily could see a glimpse of Jade's green dress move through the air. And as Lily remembered her intention for her journey to the Middle World, Jade presented herself at once to the girl.

"You," Jade shrieked as she pointed to Lily, shooting a line of fire toward her. "I hate you."

Jade stood before Lily with her hair pulled back into a tight bun, and her green claw looking nails protruded past the exterior of her fingers. She wore a long green gown which looked as though it were too heavy to wear. It was a thick velvet fabric that reached up high around her neck, almost strangling her, and Lily felt uncomfortable even looking at it.

"I'm here to release you from this world," Lily said, unsure of where the words came from, and moved slowly toward Jade, as though she held peace within her hands, ready to give it to her.

"Leave me be," Jade said as her spirit levitated above. "I don't need you! I'm loved here, and I'm wanted here."

"You're not evil. And we all love you too," Devya said, as he held his hand up with an open palm to face her. "Your body has been holding onto misplaced energy. You had a difficult life, and you held onto the pain. It began to choke you, swallow your spirit whole. It's not who you are," Devya continued as he pushed his hand forward and touched the outer edge of Jade's spirit. "You don't intend to be evil, this isn't who you are. You are pure and good energy, you are beautiful and loving and kind."

Devya clenched his fingers together as though he were holding onto something. And as he slowly moved it away from Jade, a long trail of black smoke streamed through his fingers.

"I release you from this madness," he said as he pulled the thin black rope from Jade's heart and coiled it up into a circle. "I release you. And now, may your energy be shed into something miraculous, into something beautiful. Evolve into the next great creature that you truly are."

The black cord manifested into a snake, with beady eyes and a large fat belly, and it swirled in the air by itself, turning around and around. Its mouth opened wide and began to swallow the base of its tail in one long, chomping circle. It reminded Lily of the Ouroboros, and how it was continuing to evolve and change into something new. And she wondered if that was what happened to all energy. It was constantly moving and recycling and reworking as one.

As the last of the dark energy was pulled from Jade, her entire face lightened and a sense of calmness overtook the space of where she stood. Her hair released into a soft wave of relaxed strands and the fabric of the dress upon which she wore lightened in thickness.

A sense of peace and harmony filled her entire essence, as though a loving heart could be felt beating from the inside.

"I feel like I'm opening my eyes for the very first time," Jade said, in softer tones than her usual voice.

"It's time for you to move on," Devya said as he took his wand and pointed it toward the sky. He drew a large circle, and inside it, a door appeared, opening up a portal of white light energy.

"You need to walk toward the light, the Upper World is waiting for you," Devya said as he prompted Jade to move forward.

Jade walked slowly toward the door in front of them. But before she entered through the opening, small dark clouds of black smoke drifted through the doorway. They threw themselves over Jade and cast a black shadow once more. Again, Jade turned back into the old version of herself. The hair pulled back too tightly, as though it pulled the skin from the edges of her ears. The lobes of her ears drooped down from the weight of heavy ugly earrings, and the fabric of her dress choked her slightly around her neck once more.

"You did this to me. You!" Jade screamed as she pointed at Lily and charged toward her; the memory of Jade's nice self had disappeared as quickly as it had appeared.

"Quick, take my hand," Devya said. "It's time to return."

"I call upon the energy of the Earth. To the healing vibrations of Mother Nature. Bless us with your harmony. Ground our Soul into our body as we walk with you, so that we may live presently and gracefully beneath the rising sun." Devya spoke quickly, the sound of his voice whispered over Lily's head, as she held his hands tightly.

As Devya uttered the last words, a brilliant red sun appeared in the far horizon. And as it rose high into the air, the images of Jade and the evil spirits around them began to disappear into nothingness. And when the sun rose back high above them, Lily and Devya were standing back in the ceremony ground. The Apprentices were around them chanting, and Devya still stood strumming his leaf rattle.

Lily walked over to where her body was and lay back down into it, feeling as though she had reentered into herself. When she opened her eyes, she felt a serenity of peace. Even though she had journeyed through the Middle World, which in a way was quite terrifying, the detachment she felt from her body was still present. She was overwhelmed with a feeling of calmness, a great sense of tranquility from the knowledge of her Soul being eternal.

fourteen

The Blessing

"What happened?" Lily asked sadly as she sat up on the levitating bed.

The Apprentices had wrapped a blanket around her and she was handed a clay mug of warm tea which smelled like eucalyptus. As Lily drank the tea she felt herself return completely into her body. It was as though the liquid nourished the insides of her and cemented her Soul back in its place.

"I'm sorry, Lily, but Jade wasn't ready to pass over," Devya said as he sipped upon the tea as well and sat down next to her.

"So, she's still stuck there? In the Middle World?"

"Yes, but don't be discouraged." Devya nodded, placing his hand on Lily's. "You did the best you could, and the doorway is open for her to walk through, but now it's up to her."

Lily raised her lips up slightly, trying to smile. But still, she felt like a failure.

"Why didn't she walk through?"

"Well, sometimes it's because someone in this world has not let her go yet, and that pull of wanting is so strong that it can keep a spirit tied down."

"How can I find out?" Lily asked eagerly.

Releasing Jade was the only lead she had at the moment and she had convinced herself that it could be the solution she needed to move forward. For if she could remove the evil from the world around her, perhaps she could also erase the past mistakes she had made.

"You could ask the Wise Oak Tree? It's in Naja, on the sixth land. Or perhaps the Najatinis might know."

"The Najatinis? I've heard their name before," Lily replied, trying to think of who or where.

"Yes, the little people. They reign over the land of Naja together. They are the Third Eye of our world."

Lily felt a rush of energy jump through her body, as though all the feeling had come back at once, and she sat up quickly.

"Oh, how could I've forgotten! Marlina told me they could be the key to help the people in Praza get their power back. Perhaps they will ignite the revolution?"

Devya raised his eyebrows curiously.

"Well, the Najatini's are very powerful. They hold the gate to the inner realm of consciousness," Devya said as he picked up the remaining potion and poured it into a small bottle.

"Yes, yes, I must go there then."

"But first, will you please dine with us?" Devya asked, pointing to a long table where the Apprentices sat waiting patiently with a large feast. "It's important to close the ceremony together with gratitude and praise to the Gods."

"Of course," Lily replied, blushing slightly. "Thank you, King Devya. I'd be honored. I'm so grateful for your time."

"Just Devya, remember? We're all equal," Devya said as he handed Lily the glass jar. "This plant medicine was created for you, take it. It may be useful again."

Lily reached out to take the potion but her hands were shaking, and she smiled nervously as she held such a powerful concoction.

"Don't worry. It won't take you to the same place." Devya smiled as he rubbed her hand that held the potion. "Ask for guidance of what it is you need to know and take it when you feel ready."

"Thank you. I'm not sure if I'd have the courage to use it," Lily confessed, yet tucked the potion in her pouch just the same.

"You are courageous beyond comprehension, don't ever worry. Life will never hand you something that you cannot handle." Devya nodded and then winked. "Plus, sometimes just knowing you have the option is more powerful than actually taking it."

Lily smiled coyly, proud that Devya was so humble. His passion for equality had clearly made an impact on all of those around him, for the harmonious behavior between the Apprentices and Devya felt like a large family. And together they had created a community that Lily desperately wanted to belong to. Yet, she knew the irony of such a desire: for one, it was only men; and secondly, she couldn't imagine devoting her time to that kind of lifestyle. Still, the comfort and safety she felt from their hospitality encouraged Lily to stay longer; the feeling of complete ease had marked a strong memory in her mind, one that she would never forget. Despite their lack of words to her, their presence provided so much more value, an automatic comfort of familiarity, as though they were a family from many lifetimes before.

Lily and Devya joined the Apprentices who had been waiting patiently for their arrival. The table they sat upon was a long slab of crystal rock which hovered just lightly above the ground. Around the table were many different cushions, all with unique painted designs. Lily could see from afar that she couldn't wait to touch the fabric of the cushions, for the design on the outside had been punctured with a pattern, providing such a different texture than she had never felt before. Wide platters full of unusual cuisine in petite bites covered the table in a variety of colors. The fruits and vegetables were displayed in a way that a fine dining chef would have created, and they looked like art as opposed to basic campsite meals made by the Apprentices. In between the large plates on the table sprouted single roses, each one made of clear crystal, and they added a feminine touch to the space. It was most unusual, but to Lily it looked beautiful.

"Before we eat, I shall bless this food," Devya said as he and Lily sat on the cushions in the center of the table. "It's with great pleasure that I am to deliver the gratitude from our hearts to your hearts," Devya began as he took hold of Lily's hand on the left and one of the Apprentices on his right. Lily and the Apprentices all followed, joining hands together, and as the circle was complete, once again, Lily felt a long line of electricity flowing through them all, a buzzing energy of lightness and love. "It is because of your wisdom and respect that you enabled us to journey safely through the worlds, and I give this food as an offering to the Winds of the North, South, East, and West." Devya lifted a plate and placed it in the center of the table.

Upon doing so, each Apprentice lifted a piece of crystal from the ground and placed it around the plate. Lily was encouraged to do the same. As Devya signaled that the blessing was complete, the Apprentices all let out a great cry of laughter.

"Let us feast!" Devya said as the plates of food were handed around and the conversations grew loud.

The Apprentices were all chatting to each other, and although each spoke in different languages, they all seemed to understand what one another were saying. Lily smiled as she watched, feeling the energy of those around her in an utter state of happiness. Lily could feel as though they truly loved what they did, and it was stimulating.

Devya talked to no one and instead sat silently observing and eating slowly. Lily watched admiringly, for his authority was so subtle, and yet, she felt as though he was almost as powerful as Violetta. Finally Lily felt reassured with her absence of words in the presence of others, for it was evident that those who were the wisest spoke very little.

Lily too sat in silence and ate. But the thoughts of what had happened played out in her mind, and she relived the story over and over again. She kept analyzing every little thing, wondering how she could have changed it, or performed differently.

"Are you okay, Lily?" Devya asked, interrupting the chaos in her mind.

"I … feel … disheartened," Lily said as she let out a great sigh. "I never thought visiting Sa Neo would be this hard. Jade was the most evil person I'd ever met, but then I met Allura, and it's just gotten worse. I thought I'd been through difficult times, but I was wrong. I don't understand why the problem can't be solved."

Devya stopped his eating and placed his hand on Lily's shoulder.

"It's okay Lily, don't be so hard on yourself. The only reason it's not resolved is because there's something more that needs to be revealed. Every challenge we are faced with is an opportunity to uncover a deeper layer of ourselves, and its only when we completely understand that truth will the challenge subside. These passageways are our greatest opportunities for growth."

"But I didn't think this was my lesson to be learned."

Devya looked at Lily and smiled. His shoulder-length hair blew back from his face gently in the breeze and his eyes lowered, gazing straight into Lily's.

"Everything in your life is an opportunity to create a better version of yourself. You asked for this, you want to level up into a new you, a stronger kind of you. You want this just as much as it's coming for you."

Lily looked back at Devya, confused. There it was again, the same answers she had received before, the same advice that kept coming back, but she couldn't believe it. It was too terrible! How could she possibly find any love, acceptance, or understanding in something that was so cruel?

"When will things get easier though?" Lily sighed. But the victimizing cry wasn't hanging around for long, for Devya was quick to act.

"When you start to look at them differently. You have the ability to make this change, and the determination. You'll follow through with it, I know you will. Because if you don't, you'll stay small, and you won't live, truly live. You'll be stuck in a place of uncertainty, of madness. Is this what you want?"

"Of course not. I definitely have the desire in me to make this world a better place, I just don't know how to do it and I thought I had the answers. I thought if I'd just free Jade then the mermaids would stop being killed. The mermaids ..." Lily's voice trailed off as she recalled the net that held the mermaids captive. She was scared to return to Praza, but the only thing worse than not returning was knowing that those innocent mermaids were being held against their will for another's pleasure.

"Devya, I have one last request of you, please."

Devya nodded automatically, as though the answer was already yes before the question had begun.

"There's a magical net on the land of Praza where the mermaids are captured. How can I release it?"

Devya pulled a thin thread from his ironed robe about the size of his hand. It illuminated like the light of the moon, a sense of soul, and feminine energy. He ran the cord through the tips of his fingers several times, whispering words with each stroke. Then he placed the rope over his eyes, above his head, and over his chest. Each movement slower than the last. And finally, he circled it up tightly in a ball, squeezing it in his fist tightly.

"Although we can't get involved, I can give you this to make a difference. We can all help you in some way, just not always in the way that you want," Devya said as he handed Lily the ball of rope. "Open the rope tightly with both hands, and use it like a saw; it will cut through that net in an instant."

Lily graciously accepted the gift and felt the vibrations of freedom liberate her body as though the task had already been done.

"I must go now while it is dark," Lily said and gobbled down the last of her plate.

"It's not dark in Praza, we're the opposite side. Lay down to rest here, and I will awaken you when it's time to leave, okay?" Devya said as he stood up and walked Lily to a bed made up for her to rest.

Lily went to sleep that night feeling a mixture of emotions. Slowly she was finding the answers to help solve her problems, but she felt as though the deeper she dug, the greater the hole grew that needed to be filled. And perhaps that's the reason why so many people gave up, she thought. Because it was a great big mess when someone finally did start to uncover the truth. This led to that and that to this. And even when she thought she had all the answers to solve the problem, things kept happening to distract her on her journey. But then again, Lily rationalized in her mind that she could look at it both ways. If she reflected on the journey she was being guided along the way. Something kept pushing her in the right direction, and she had no other option than to believe that each step was necessary in creating the final masterpiece that she was working toward. *Bit by bit.* She heard the words echo in her mind. And as she drifted peacefully off to sleep, she felt strong in her decision, in the next steps. She would free the mermaids, and then go to Naja, and find the Wise Oak Tree.

fifteen

The Power of One

Lily arrived on the orange-pebbled shores of Praza as the three moons rose high in the sky. On the beach, the water gushed over the small pebbles, throwing itself fearlessly over them, only to chase themselves back to where they came from. Some water decided to leave the ocean, opting to bathe beneath the sun instead and disappear up into the sky. It wanted to become something different to how it was before. Lily thought about the great beauty of the water being able to change into another identity. She reflected on how it referred to her life. How energy was constantly reforming back into something new and yet could recreate into what it was. The ideas played in Lily's mind as she walked along the windy pathway back into the village. She walked over the ponds, and high along the bridges. She heard a loud croaking noise from below and she stopped to look down. There before her lay hundreds of beautiful blood-orange frogs lazing on the rocks, gleefully living off the splashes from the waterfalls nearby. All shapes and sizes, *they looked like they were having a party,* she thought.

Lily arrived to the village shortly after and crept quietly through the streets. The village purred in silence, a soft drumming heartbeat of deep breathing. Lily could feel as though everyone had wandered off into their dreams, dancing through the night. Lily walked through the town and past the fountain until she reached the edge of the forest. It appeared completely full of life in contrast to the sleepy village that she had just left. The trees hung down low, and she could see fireflies streaming above, like fireworks, commending, celebrating. Lily smiled. They felt untouchable. So high up in the air. Alight for a moment and then they disappeared. Like shooting stars.

Except they kept appearing and reappearing, and she felt as though she was given a second chance to make a wish. A second chance to make things right.

To the far left Lily could make out a small mushroom ring with fairies, playing around and having a tea party. She crept closer to the edges of the woods and watched as the miniature cut-out people that looked like her tiny dolls as a child all played together. They drank out of flower drops, and flew hurriedly around in circles, chasing one another. Their games were as childlike as their demeanor. Lily thought about how wonderful it must've been to never grow up and stay in that mind-frame as a child forever. Forever learning and forever playing.

When Lily turned back around she could see in the distance a light flickering and as she walked closer she realized that it was the bonfire from the full moons gathering. Lily carefully checked that no one was around and then entered the ceremony space, but she felt a strange emptiness as soon as she did so. There had been another sacrifice. A mermaid was killed. She knew it. She could feel it. It was a disturbing feeling. And yet Lily still felt responsible. It reminded her of her connection to the two worlds. How she wished she could ignite them together, and yet she had pushed them even further apart. *How was it possible to create peace in a land of chaos? Where people are manipulated into fear, and war, and hatred, and killing. How can I show them that there is another way?* Lily wondered as she walked as close to the fire as possible.

The fire burned brightly, and in small explosions, the flames leapt into the air. Lily could stare into the center for hours, mesmerized from the memories of times gone past, and anticipation of what could be from the future. The longer she stared, the more enchanted the flames became with her, and they soon began to dance for her. She watched enamored as it exploded up amongst the stars, and she once again was brought back into that moment. A moment of joy, laughter, and love.

Lily looked down to the ground to search for any ruins left over. She pushed her hands through the ashes and sifted them lightly through her fingers. And upon doing so, she felt the mermaids from before. There were many.

"Show me the necklace," Lily recited in her head, opening her hands to feel a pull of strength as to which direction she was to follow.

And a pull she felt indeed, but the energy was pulling her closer toward the fire, and it pulled on her chest, drastically. She opened her eyes and looked beneath the flames, for there, under a black coal of darkness, lay a cluster of Ouroboros necklaces, almost a hundred of them.

Lily felt as though a dagger had pierced through her heart and carved it open. And her heart was bleeding uncontrollably with shame and regret for not coming back sooner. The questions of 'what if' were circling her mind, for perhaps if she had returned earlier the world would not be in the madness that it were now. *How dare I believe that this world was not real?* Lily thought as she began to breathe in short breaths, feeling herself drown within her own sorrow. It was as though she had swum back inside the waters of her depression once more. Yet she knew she was the one responsible for jumping back in. *Why am I doing this to myself?* She asked.

Lily sat on the ground and touched the ashes in-between her fingers once more. And with a small cup nearby she filled it with the ashes, and in her free hand, carried the Ouroboros necklaces. Determined to make things right. She had one choice, and it was to keep going. How she hated the feeling of fear, regret, and sadness. It had been a long time since such a heartache had knocked at her door, and she couldn't help but feel responsible for allowing such darkness back in. She felt as though she was the one who not only opened the door but was the one who knocked. Could she be the one responsible for both?

Lily walked back to the ocean holding the ashes of the mermaids who had passed. The moons above shone brightly in the sky. They were no longer full, they were a crescent moon, as though the eyes of the moon were crying for her too. And with a heavy heart she walked into the water, tipping the ashes of those who had passed on back to the world upon which they came from.

"I release you," Lily whispered as the ashes flew far over the water, moving like glittering stars twinkling in the night sky.

Next, she pulled out the Ouroboros necklaces that she had found on the ceremony ground. As Lily touched the charms she felt as though she could feel the sheer terror that the mermaids' experienced as their lives were ripped from them. She thought back to all the creatures in her life that were innocently killed. It was the reason she had become vegan, she couldn't bear the thought of an animal screaming for morality in the last moments of its life. And how that screaming and pain energy would then be embedded into something for her to consume inside her own body. She felt sick even thinking of it. No wonder the world was going crazy when people were eating flesh from another, forgetting that it could've been from their own kin. *How can a race feel so superior to not value another creature's life? Who gave them that right?* she wondered. Lily could feel not only the sadness that the mermaids had faced but also the misery in the village folk who were made to watch. The feelings of being obliged to go along with something despite an internal struggle of anger, of wanting something to be different, and yet also the anguish of not speaking up.

But finally, now was the time to tell the mermaids that safety was coming. Now was the time to repair the friendship that once was. She was to declare a new agreement, a safe world of peace. There was nothing to be feared.

Lily dangled the necklaces into the ocean's edge as she thought about her message to be shared. A long silver stream oozed from Lily's hand into the far horizon, and upon doing so, Lily closed her eyes. She envisioned a line of communication that connected her to Indigo and within moments she could feel his energy. She imagined his ink eyes upon her, his beautiful silver-and-black hair, and his masculine body of strength.

"Indigo, come to the shore of Praza." Lily whispered through the wire as the words echoed through the ocean, rippling the waves above.

"Indigo, come to the shores of Praza," she chanted in her mind. And as she did so, she imagined the love and safety that was present in her heart for him. It was her way of letting him know that he had nothing to fear. After several more chants she lifted the necklaces back up and sat on the water's edge. But still she didn't give up; she had faith that he would arrive.

Indigo's eyes pierced through the water before he surfaced, and like a shark lurking beneath, he watched above, indecisive as to whether she was prey. Lily held his gaze, pleading through her mind, telling him he had to talk to her.

"You again," Indigo replied as he hovered above the water, his long hair slicked casually over one eye. "How did you call me without the Ouroboros?"

"This is for you, I'm so sorry," Lily said as she showed Indigo the cluster of necklaces in her hand. "I know my words can never erase what has happened, but I ask for your forgiveness."

Indigo didn't look at the necklaces and continued to stare at Lily. He displayed his warrior face erasing any emotion that he may have felt.

"Do you forgive yourself?" he finally said, his eyes piercing through her skin.

Lily bowed her head in reply, she wasn't sure how to answer that question, and she changed the subject awkwardly. "I have a plan to overthrow the Queen; there will be no more murders, your merpeople can live in peace, safely in these waters. You have my word."

Indigo rolled his eyes and raised his eyebrows mockingly.

"And you think your word is going to save us all?" Indigo said as he tossed his head to the side, dismissing Lily.

"If I don't have my word, what else do I have?" Lily pleaded with him.

With every inhale she felt as though she were breathing his energy, his aura, and that it was bringing her closer to him. She couldn't help but feel a strange attachment. A strong pull embedded from years ago. It was the feeling of seeing an old friend, the memories, although disjointed, still felt so alive and real as though they happened a few moments ago.

"Your actions. It's the reason we are all like this in the first place. It's because of you that we now have to hide in our waters. It's because of your word and your actions that I'm now a hunter. That I live with constant pressure to protect my community. That I have to kill for a lifestyle choice. But I didn't get this choice. This decision was made for me." Indigo moved closer to Lily now, and he rose above the water, displaying his body fiercely. "I'm the strongest and bravest merman in all of Neosa and I'm the one responsible for hundreds of thousands of lives. I hate you for what you have done to me. I hate that I have blood on my hands because of you."

Indigo grunted with anger as he subsided back down into the water. But despite his intimidation act, Lily could see that his eyes held great sadness between them, the weight of carrying this burden around his whole life.

"Indigo, I wish I could take it all away," Lily tried again, although as she said the words out loud she realized that they weren't entirely true. For if she didn't visit Sa Neo, Mia Veol would never have been freed, and what about Silvia? She still had yet to find out, but she hoped that her friend had escaped her servant life.

"I'm here to make this wrong right, Indigo. Believe me, my heart is broken for the hardship you've endured," Lily said again, now picking the fabric between her dress, and pressing the edges lightly. A coping defense mechanism that she once used as a child. Now she was using it for strength, instead of an opportunity for distraction. "This is why I brought these to you, to show you an offering of peace. I didn't know before, but I understand now, and I'm sorry. I'm trying to fix it," Lily said as tears surfaced in her eyes and in her hands, she felt as though she was holding tortured Souls and painful energy, a disturbing feeling of anguish and fear weighed heavily in the chains.

Indigo stared at Lily with no words. His hair flopped on one side, and the pointed tips of the fringe dripped down his cheek. The jawline of his chin was strong, and he breathed deeply in his chest. Indigo lifted his hand and pushed the hair back from his face so he could look Lily directly in the eyes. And as before, Lily felt a magnetic pull between them. An unusual desire to learn more about him.

As Lily handed over the necklaces and touched Indigo's hands, a jolt of electricity sizzled between the two of them, splashing the water high into the sky.

"Did you feel that?" Lily asked, holding her hand and regaining her breath.

But Indigo didn't reply, his energy was suffocated with the charms he held in his hands.

"Do you know about fisherman's corner?" Lily asked, trying to get through to him again. "There's a silver net in the sea of Praza where the merpeople have been getting caught. It's invisible to the eye and it's cast as far as imaginable. I have a weapon to cut through it and I'm going to destroy it. Do you trust me?"

Indigo opened his lips lightly, ready to speak. But something held him back.

"Will you meet me near there? When the net is cut there'll be many merpeople who'll need guidance to go back home. They need your help. I need your help."

Indigo looked at Lily, his eyes squinting slightly, wondering if he could trust her. But Lily didn't wait for a response, she needed to act fast.

"I'll run and meet you there," Lily said, as she turned around and quickly bolted through the forest, past the village, and along the path to the fisherman's corner.

sixteen

Connected by Love

Lily covered her nose from the smell of rotting fish as she arrived to the broken ship at the fisherman's corner.

"The eagle." she heard a voice inside her speak, and out of the corner of her eye she could see the bird watching her every move. Within moments, Lily rubbed the amethyst ring and said a prayer, creating a magic bubble of invisibility around herself. But still, there were those few moments she had forgotten, and so she moved hurriedly, nervous that the fishermen and their horses would arrive any second.

Indigo was nowhere to be seen, but still, Lily stayed focused. She ran up to the edge of the boat and peered over, seeing the tortured mermaids and mermen barely conscious. Lily swallowed hard and took a deep breath as she fastened the rope from Devya tightly between her two hands and began to carve at the net. But as she started to slice through each piece of web she felt the bodies weigh heavier, and now, not only could she see the repercussions of her actions once more, she could feel it too. There was no denying what had happened—pure evil had erupted through the world. Tears pushed through her eyes and slid down her cheeks, falling hopelessly into the ocean below. She desperately tried to hold back her whimpering cries with each thread of the net that she cut through. As the last piece was set free a giant splash erupted into the water as the mermaids were finally liberated and they looked to each other, confused as to what had actually happened. Some swam quickly, desperate to escape such a torturous death again, others were in a state of shock, and some were on the final edges of their life, floating near the top of the water.

Lily peered over the edge as she watched the mer-people trying to survive, taking the floating bodies back down below. She wished so badly that there was something more that she could do. And she stared into the water, hoping to see Indigo again.

The eagle was flying up high in the air, watching over the fisherman's edge. In the distance Lily could hear the sound of horses galloping and she looked back to the pathway to see if she was in danger. The leaves on the trees were swaying back and forth as though interrupted with something, and there were birds flying above wanting to get away from whatever it was.

"Lily, thank you."

Lily turned back around to see a humbled Indigo with his hands in prayer. It was the most vulnerable Lily had ever seen him, and in a split moment she could feel his remorse and caring heart beating loudly.

"Thank you for coming." Lily replied, looking to the water at the last of the mermaids.

"They're coming." Indigo said as he pointed behind her to the fishermen on horses who were drawing close. "Come with us," he continued as he held his hand out to her.

Lily could see in the far corner of her eye the fishermen's horses galloping toward them, and the sound of their hooves thumping against the ground. She didn't think too long and took hold of Indigo's hand quickly, immersing herself into the ocean. The moment her body touched the water she felt an immediate sense of calmness overtake her senses, like she had finally returned to where she belonged. She looked down to her body, what was once her teenage legs was now a beautiful long white tail. Everything came back to her mind easily. They way she glided beneath the water, swimming as though she was born to be a mermaid. The ease of breathing underwater, the luscious vibrations of sea salt softening against her skin.

"Come," Indigo said, still holding onto her hand and pulling her alongside him, his black eyes staring at her body. "We must take them to heal."

The other merpeople had all dispersed into the water by now, and Lily could see the tips of their fins swimming in the far distance.

"Are we going to the Kingdom?" Lily asked, remembering the beautiful seashell castle she visited last time.

"It's no longer there," Indigo replied solemnly, looking straight ahead and continuing to swim. "The witches bombed our homes; they also hit the edge of the Ball of Neo, but then the winds above changed and they stopped. For they had disrupted the harmonious balance of the world."

"Indigo, I'm so sorry. I had no idea."

"I tried to tell you." Indigo said as he continued to look straight ahead but in this moment, his eyes darted quickly to the side, gauging Lily's reaction.

"In my dreams? They were real weren't they?" Lily asked, remembering the energy that she felt when she touched Indigo's hands both in Sa Neo and in the dreams, they were identical.

"I lied when I said I didn't remember you." Indigo replied as he peeked his eyes to the side back at Lily. "My memory of you was that of an angel, entwined to my spirit from lifetimes before. You're the only one who I can call upon and connect with from the outside world."

Lily tried to see more of Indigo's face as he spoke for the first time kindly toward her. But his eyes were fixated ahead, still holding himself strong. As though that split moment of his heart opened was now closed back up.

"We're here." Indigo said as they stopped in front of a cave and pushed his chest out, taking his strong stance once again.

Lily wanted to talk more about their connection and ask what it really meant. Whether he felt a pull of energy as well, or shared the same comfort of being near one another, a desire to learn more. But she stopped herself, it was clear that the moment had gone.

"This is the only good thing that came from our Kingdom falling, we found this place," Indigo said as he led Lily inside. "We have lived in these seas since the beginning of time, and yet this cave had remained untouched until now."

The moment they passed through the opening of the cave, an entire world like no other appeared before them. Amidst the darkness were electrical lights from the tips of the seaweed sashaying from side to side, illuminating the entire cave. Large glowing starfish clung to the walls and radiated a rainbow of lights around them all. Even the texture of the water felt different inside the cave, it was soft to touch and cool against Lily's skin. The fresh temperature awoke Lily's senses in a way she had never felt before, and a shooting of energy in the highest vibration imaginable pulsated over her body and in her mind. The lights, the vibrations, the textures was an overload of sensory explosion and Lily loved every minute of it.

"Will you join our circle?" Indigo's voice brought Lily back into her mermaid body, and the euphoric high that she was breathing through the water had subsided as she joined the other merpeople who had created a circle around those who were caught in the net.

Three mermaids and one merman lay in the middle. They were lined up next to one another on a crystal table similar to the one in Deia, although this one had an illuminated light that seeped above their bodies, as though protecting them. Lily took hold of Indigo's hand on her left, and another mermaid's hand on her right, and together they prayed.

"That's Saffyr," Indigo whispered as an elderly mermaid stepped forth into the circle, and with one hand on her heart, and the other hand hovered above the sickly mermaids and merman, she walked around. The circle of merpeople holding hands began to sing, no words, just harmonic sounds of high and low tones. Each note completely different, yet somehow joined together to play as one. And as the soft singing of the merpeople grew louder, the old lady walked faster, pulling sickness from their bodies, and discarding it above.

The sound of the merpeople's voices now moved from their mouths in a stream of rainbow-colored lights which followed Saffyr, moving deep within her heart, and through her hands. The energy she pulled from the sick bodies was a muddy green color, and as it rose above them, the water took control, and eroded the mass into tiny little particles, as though suffocating the illness with the cleanliness of vibrant breath.

"I call upon the spirit of our ancestors, come forth. Carry our loved ones to life, or take them to death. Remove them from misery," Saffyr said as she looked above.

Within moments ghostly beings hovered over the circle. The image of what they were was too hard to see, it appeared as just a shimmer of light, but the feeling they exuded was thickly present. It encompassed a sensation of peace, the feeling of knowing, and the blessings of eternal glory. As Lily looked at the shadow shapes, she would see glimpses of their bodies outlined, but only for a moment, for then they would return to themselves, a ball of light and fire. The ancestors twirled around the circle, breathing love from their souls toward the group. Saffyr stood still and closed her eyes as the breath from the ancestors breathed into her, using her body as their tool. She began to walk again, her eyes still closed, and she moved to the closest lying mermaid. She touched the forehead, cradling the crown with her hand, and pulling it gently. The mermaid who was lying on the table suddenly opened her mouth and gasped a great breath. Her eyes opened wide as she was pulled through from her chest to sit upright. The merpeople continued to sing, and Saffyr moved on to the next ill-fated creature; it was the merman who lay there. Once again, Saffyr placed her hand on the crown and pulled gently; the energy from the ancestors above swirled through Saffyr's body, and nudged the merman with a breath of air. He too sat up and gasped with a great breath.

Again, Saffyr moved to the next, another mermaid. The ancestors blew their energy with strength through Saffyr, and she stood up high on the tip of her fin as she bent over to touch the forehead. But this time the mermaid did not gasp for air, and instead, Lily saw the soul of the mermaid rise from her chest up high above to the crowd of ancestors. And here, Lily saw the shape of their bodies take form once more; with open arms and a loving heart they welcomed the mermaid into their chamber of safety. Still, the merpeople did not stop singing, and Saffyr moved to the final mermaid. The ancestors twirled around once more above, and with all their energy pushed through Saffyr; with her hand on the forehead, the final mermaid gasped with air and sat upright.

The ancestors who were hovering above took the mermaid who had passed and disappeared as the other merpeople rushed forward to comfort those who had survived. Saffyr opened her eyes exhausted and collapsed into a group of mermen who lifted her and carried her onto the same table to relax and regain consciousness.

Indigo turned to Lily; his armor of protection had lowered around his heart once more and he spoke sincerely. "Thank you for being here with us."

Lily looked back to him. Despite her relief that the mermaids were released she still felt displaced, yet in that moment of looking at Indigo, everything else faded away. He made her feel different, like nothing else mattered anymore.

"It was my honor to share it with you." The words finally came out of Lily's mouth, but she feared she had spent too long looking into his eyes, that perhaps he felt something more too. But if Indigo shared her emotional tie he did not show it, for his armor of protection covered his stance once more.

"I'll take you back to shore."

"I need to go to the land of Naja, it's the sixth land, with dark-blue crystals; do you know it?"

Indigo nodded, looking away to the exit of the cave.

"That land is our favorite. The Najatinis are unharmed by the rules of society around them."

"Well, apparently that's where I'll find the answers. They hold the gate to our inner realm of consciousness, and they have the answers to changing this world."

"I'll take you there." Indigo said as he took hold of Lily's hand and held onto it tightly. Not once did he look back at her, although she was sure that he felt her gaze upon him.

Within moments, Lily was standing on the shore of Naja. She was completely dry, dressed in a floral skirt and top, and holding her pouch bag, but this time, she had her Ouroboros necklace fastened around her neck.

"I'm going to make this right, Indigo. I promise," Lily said as she held the necklace, thanking him for its safe return.

Indigo nodded quickly, and he turned away, diving deep below the ocean. Lily couldn't help but desperately ache for his approval, yet at the same time she could empathize with what he was thinking. To him, she was a foolish, innocent girl, one who didn't realize the depth of the world around her. And now that she did, she was changing it, but the will alone was not enough, she needed to take action. The desire to change the world's evil ways needed to be fulfilled for her conscience, but there was something deep within, something in the unconscious, something that tied her heart to Indigos, that made her want to succeed even more. The desire for his blessing, his understanding, his friendship. It's all she could think about, for she so badly wanted to see him again.

seventeen

The Wise Old Oak Tree

Lily touched the dark-blue crystals on the beach of Naja as the sun rose high in the sky. The ocean before her was now very calm, with almost non-existent waves, and they purred lightly against the shore, drifting back and forth in peace. Along the edge of the beach was a thick forest of trees. It appeared to be more dense than any of the other lands that Lily had visited. The trees were short but very thick, and the branches touched each other, crossing over to create a bridge. Because the majority of trees were quite short, Lily could see one grand tree in the distance and she knew immediately that it was "The Wise Oak Tree." She walked quickly toward it, following an open pathway that appeared.

The density of the forest aroused Lily. The magnitude of beauty that it held was overbearingly heavy to absorb all at once. It needed to be done in small portions. The ground, the way the patterns in the dirt told stories of their past. The trees, such marvelous ancient creations standing tall, thousands of years old. *If only I could see what they had seen,* she thought. The leaves blew gently down to the ground like shooting stars, each one carrying a wish, a dream, that would soon be forgotten.

As Lily walked, she reflected over her time in Sa Neo. She felt a mixture of feelings, yes; she had released the captured mermaids, but the problem of inequality still existed. She needed to persuade the people of Praza to stand up for themselves, not be led astray by evil from their lack of self-worth; she needed to convince them of their own power. She still had things to figure out. But at least she was on the right track, in the land of Naja, and ready to ask for help from the Wise Oak Tree.

The pathway that guided Lily was covered in colored hues of blue petals that sheathed the flooring. Lily felt inclined to take off her shoes to let the sweet smell stain the soles of her feet, and she did so hurriedly, desperate to touch the softness on her skin. Little blue flying creatures hovered down low as she walked, some were tiny fairies, and others were small dragonflies. When Lily stopped on her path, she could hear the buzzing of animals near her. A giant peacock walked out in front of Lily. It turned to her and opened its feathers wide, displaying a tremendous artwork of patterns. The eyes of the feathers were a bright white, and they contrasted against the dark blue eyelash tips. It was a marvelous sight to see. The printed feathers were both on the front as well as the back, and the peacock turned around to show off, as though encouraging Lily to keep moving forward. To which Lily, of course, did.

One of the beautiful feathers dropped to the floor, and Lily picked it up, waving it in front of her. As she did so, a line of sparkles fell from the feather and onto the pathway ahead. It moved forward in a line, a sign once again encouraging Lily to keep walking. Everything around Lily was pushing her down this path, and magnetically toward the Wise Oak Tree. Lily followed the blue-and-white feathered peacock until she finally reached the magnificent glowing tree.

The Wise Oak Tree stood taller than any tree Lily had ever seen. It reached up high into the clouds, and its arms stretched for miles, with hundreds of them swaying gently in the breeze. It was complete daylight and yet the tree was glowing in pulsating vibrations. The leaves on the edges of the branches looked like small teardrops encasing shining stars, and they fell slowly down like raindrops full of sparkling lights. The leaves hovered, magically just next to the branch, circling around, an endless flow of energy as though it were connected by an invisible force. A soft humming noise moved through the sparkling leaves, creating a beautifully sounding "om" as they danced around merrily. Lily felt her body become lighter as she walked closer to the heavenly tree. With each step forward, the exterior background around her just melted into a blur. Nothing else mattered. As she gazed upon the Wise Oak Tree, the outside world did not exist, it was purely only herself and the angelic tree.

A moat of sparkling blue water surrounded the tree, as though it were a protective barrier, stopping anyone coming too close. Small lizards bathed in the water, drinking from the lake. Blue swans and ducks swam in the water too, and more butterflies flew overhead. The peacock that led Lily joined five other birds that were there as well, and they pecked on the ground together, picking at the soil between the petals.

Lily felt as though she was surrounded within a place of peace and worship and great power of ancestral wisdom. As she looked to the bark, the lines that cracked along the body resembled that of skin. The tree was not merely a tree: it was an entity, a form of energy that had a wise Soul, that had lived on for many years. Lily looked over the edge of the water. The stream ran clear, and the crystals below reminded Lily of the dream, how they shone too brightly, blocking her vision to see the land properly. Within the water, Lily could see fish and turtles swimming. The water extended incredibly deeply below the surface, and if Lily squinted her eyes she could see as though the entire surface upon which she stood was water too. It was as though the two elements of land and water molded into one. Below the water at a distance Lily thought that she could see the mermaids giggling, dancing, and holding hands. And above the water around the tree appeared ghostly shadows of dancing females, holding hands and swaying from side to side. Hints of sweet giggling whispered through the trees around them. Even though it was Lily and the animals and no one else, she knew she was not alone.

Lily found a small spot on the edge of the river bank to sit down. It was a thick landing full of petals that layered up lightly like a hill, creating a soft seat. She took her bag off and looked to the tree, enamored in its presence.

Lily leaned over and gently touched the water between her fingers. The water felt soft and calming. Lily ached to bathe within the water herself. And she wondered if it was possible. Whether anything magical would happen.

"Dear Wise Oak ..." Lily began feeling a need to voice her concerns, "There is great danger on the land of Praza and I need your help."

The ghostly women who danced around the tree appeared in definition, and they sashayed in a vibrant movement upon hearing Lily's voice.

"Why is there danger?" they asked together in one long, chiming sound as they let go of their hands, now each turning toward Lily. There were five of them.

"Because of Queen Allura. She is killing mermaids to start a war. There is no reason for such evil."

"There is a reason," the women chanted again, taking a step closer to Lily. "Look into the water and see the truth."

Lily obeyed and moved closer to the edge of the water. She leaned over slightly and peered at the reflection. The water swirled in a large circle. It seemed to navigate in a fluid motion, around and around. The color of the water spun so quickly it started to resemble that of the galaxy, as it mirrored the lights in the tree above. The shadow angels moved closer to Lily, and they crouched down, looking Lily deeply in the eyes as she stared at the lake.

"Deep breaths, sweet girl," the voices said in an eerie echo. "All will be revealed."

Lily blinked as she inhaled deeply, and the water began to calm down. As it did, the reflection of the world stood still. And Lily's face staring back at her was in clear sight. Lily looked at the lake and back to the angels.

"But ... I," Lily stuttered, and she touched the top of her fingernails, remembering the hardness of her nail to bring her back to reality.

But it didn't work.

The angels all laughed in Lily's face as they floated back to the tree and held each other's hands.

"You." They laughed again as they twirled in their dances once more.

Lily stared into the river at the girl who looked back her. Tears formed in Lily's eyes and they crept away from her, crawling down her face, as though desperate to dive into the water that she stared into. It was her. How could she forget for a moment that she was the one who did this? The tears that Lily bled couldn't help save the massacred mermaids. And she wiped her face hurriedly, breathing in strength from deep inside her heart center.

"Show me how to fix this," Lily asked assertively as she removed her self-pity and replaced it with strength.

A vision of Indigo formed in front of her with his daring eyes staring deeply into her Soul. And his words—"Have you forgiven yourself?"—played over repeatedly in her head.

Lily knew this all along. But she still hadn't acknowledged that it happened and let it go. She hadn't taken full responsibility for the change that had flowed from her doing; she hadn't let the energy move through her. Every turn she took in Sa Neo proved to her that the world had changed because of her actions, but instead of focusing on the good that had come of it, she was staring at the sadness, holding onto the past, unable to let it go.

Lily looked back to the floating angelic creatures. They twirled so beautifully, like giddy children, rushing around with great excitement. Almost oblivious to Lily's attendance.

"Help me solve this," Lily pleaded, shouting over the giggling angels.

"Forgive yourself ..."

Lily heard the words resonate within her but she couldn't do it. She felt responsible. The story of her past that she told herself echoed back in her mind. Her first visit to the world of Sa Neo was her greatest achievement and her greatest regret at the same time. *How is it possible that I've created such madness and such beauty at the same time?* she wondered.

"Help me heal this world," Lily pleaded again, now feeling a rise of emotions stir within herself. They twirled around in her head, replicating the dancing angels in front of her.

"Show the world your true self," the angels whispered as they moved faster and faster around the tree.

Lily sat backward on the ground as the epiphany of their words cemented an internal eruption. She nodded with agreement, stunned that she couldn't see it for what it was. It was true. She had been hiding who she really was, unable to face the blame for what had happened and yet her sole basis of starting a revolution was based on the fact that those around her weren't being true to themselves and standing up for what they believed in. Despite the fact that she herself was still cowering, hiding in fear of being wrongfully judged. She needed to expose herself in order to expose the truth for what had happened. It all finally made sense.

It was exactly as Violetta had foretold: she first had to acknowledge the situation and then forgiveness. She had confronted her fears but not forgiven herself, for she still held great regret for what she had done. And with the angelic creatures dancing around Lily in a beautiful, loving harmony, she realized how simple her life could be if she just relaxed, went with the flow of the universe, and forgave herself.

Lily looked again to the reflection of herself in the water. She felt as though a magnetic vibration was energetically pulling her to the center, and she stared with amazement, with wonder.

"I forgive you," Lily said as she looked at the girl in the reflection.

And upon the words being repeated, the edges of her face rippled from the water. Leaving only her eyes to stare at. Lily's eyes were beautiful, dark green iris with slithers of black scratches, yet sometimes she forgot to notice them. But when she uttered the forgiveness to herself she finally saw them in a different light, as something remarkable. The greens of her eyes reminded her of nature with their incredible rich beauty. The dense rainforest near her house that she liked to explore. And the small streaks of black that tickled the edges, how wonderfully the colors in her eyes balanced the weight of light and dark in perfect harmony. She remembered how sometimes when she was upset or angry, how dark her eyes could become. But in this moment as she completely surrendered with no thoughts, no worries, no questions or answers, her eyes had changed into a beautiful lightness. The lightness had taken over her body and she exhaled softly. Feeling the air gradually move through her body, pushing her stomach in and out. She had never felt so much at peace at this exact moment of looking at herself. And yet she still had a difficult time recognizing herself in these moments. The body, her face, the exterior, it didn't define who she was; she felt as though it was merely a shell that encased the truth, an abundance of light.

The dancing angels rejoined hands once more and continued to dance around the tree. Lily sat on the shore watching them for a while, watching their bodies move with grace. They moved in a long stream, waving their arms toward another path behind where Lily was sitting. The rose petals turned into thick blue leaves, and Lily felt destined to move forward, but first, she needed to find out about Jade.

"If I tell the people what I did, will Jade finally cross over? Will it release her from here?" Lily asked, hoping that it would be true.

"Jade resides in the Middle World, the lands of broken promises, hopes, and dreams. She floats through the lands lost, creating havoc around her being ..." the voices echoed as they moved back and forth in their dance-like state. "When a Soul opens their mind to negative thoughts, it's an opportunity for her to enter. She brings them reasons to hate life, to destroy the idea of happiness. For where death grows, hurt, anger, and pain live on, and this is where she is able to survive."

Lily shuddered at the mere thought of what a terrible world had been created instead of the one she had left.

"How can she leave this world and pass on?"

"As long as there is still someone who wants her alive, she will stay."

"Who wants her alive?"

The angels smiled as they twirled around. A bizarre movement of dancing and lights and music that hummed through the trees.

"You do."

Lily screamed.

"I don't believe it. It's not true, it's not true," Lily yelled back as she shook her head abruptly.

But it was of no use, the spirits laughed at her pity. And they mocked her in her tears. Lily jumped up quickly; grabbing her bag, she ran away from the ghostly angels, and followed along the path of blue petals and floating fairies.

eighteen

The Najatinis

Lily ran as fast as her legs would carry her as the singing angels continued to haunt her from afar. Their voices whispered through the air in soft muffles and over the trees above following her footsteps. *Why would I want that horrid person still alive?* Lily thought as she ran. And she ran and ran until she found herself in the middle of a field full of tall blue flowers, far away from the chilling sounds. In this field the flowers grew past Lily's knees almost up to her waist and the smell was unlike anything Lily had smelled from a flower before. It wasn't the usual floral scent, nor the smell of fruits, but a strange spicy aroma, the kind of smell one would like to cook with. Lily stopped and sat down, out of breath, and admired the strange life of the flowers in front of her.

Unsure where her desire had come from, she pulled the flowers from the ground and began to weave the pieces together to create a crown. As she wove each thread of a flower through, Lily asked for guidance from Violetta and imagined the beautiful empress in front of her. The moment she called upon Violetta she appeared. But not standing in front of her, in her body; instead, Lily saw a floating purple light, hovering just above the crown. Lily felt as though it was Violetta's Soul traveling through to her.

"I am creating this crown to weave your support into the world. I know you cannot get involved, nor do you want to. But that doesn't mean I cannot wish for your help. I feel stronger knowing that there is the possibility of you by my side."

Lily recalled the memory of looking at the baby that Violetta had held in her hands. It was a beautiful innocent child who had arrived in this world with no idea of what fear meant, no idea what it meant to be suppressed for being different. And from that reflection, Lily realized that her role in the world was to create a better place for every unborn child, so that the next generation could live in peace and harmony. For every action she created had the potential to pave the way for a better future.

And so Lily continued to weave her thoughts and desires into the crown. With each twig and flower that she wove, she imagined as though she was threading the strength and courage of everyone around her, symbolizing the unity and connection within the collective unconscious. And as Lily did so, she imagined she was communicating with everyone she had met in the world. She was envisioning that they were all supporting her and wanting her to lead the people to make this change.

The words of Devya from Deia moved through her body next and she felt an overwhelming sense of clarity in her communication. From the simple shift of tuning into her heart she had cleared the passageway for her voice to come through. An image of Mia Veol flashed in her mind next and her wonderful gift of balancing Lily's feminine and masculine energies. As Lily placed the last piece of blue flower through the crown Lily felt the strength of all the leaders she had met supporting her journey. But then Lily thought about the Wise Oak Tree, and their words. *How could I be the reason that Jade was still alive? Why would I want her alive?* she wondered. But instead of playing the victim as she usually did, she decided to rephrase the question by twisting the words around and understanding the sentence from a different point of view: If Jade were still alive then … And that's when Lily realized the truth.

"If Jade were still alive, that would mean that I never hurt anyone. That no one ever died because of me, that my actions didn't spark a war between the witches and the mermaids. If Jade were still alive, I wouldn't hold this deep regret in my heart." As Lily spoke the words out loud a violent thunder shook within her core.

She felt the whole world spin around her completely and hurriedly. And her mind twirled with dizziness. She closed her eyes, blinking them quickly as a great downpour of tears flooded through her hands. "But it's time to let you go. I release you." Lily continued as she cried, holding her head in her hands.

As the tears moved through her fingers and into the ground below she felt as though the release of water was washing her Soul and a gift of clarity and wisdom was emerging in its place. She felt stronger because of it, and never before had her tears created such a moment of profound growth.

"Why are you crying?" a squeaky voice interrupted Lily.

Lily looked up to see a small child whose head now parted through the tops of the flowers. The child had thin blue hair that was tied up high into a tight bun, and three small stars painted across its forehead.

"I've come from the Wise Oak Tree," Lily said as she straightened up her hair and blinked her eyes dry.

"Ah, I see. You weren't ready to accept the truth, huh?" The little child smiled, showing three big teeth protruding from its gums.

"Yes. But I understand now." Lily swallowed hard, fighting a smile to push through. The moment she did, she felt better. There was something endearing about being in the presence of the child. Lily didn't want to show them the feeling of pain or sadness, their innocence was too pure. "Look, I made this flower crown, do you like it?"

"Oh, it's wonderful! Put it on, will you?" the little child replied, clapping their hands quickly, to which Lily placed the crown on her head. "They really are the most beautiful blue flowers you've ever seen, right?" the blue-haired child continued as it pointed to the flowers.

"Yes, they really are mesmerizing," Lily replied, looking at the child, now wondering if it were a boy or a girl.

"They are the eyes of the world, did you know?" the child replied, stepping forward to reveal denim overalls and a long-sleeved blue shirt. It gave no indication as to its gender, and it didn't matter to Lily. For their heart felt pure, full of love and peace.

"What do you mean by the eyes of the world?" Lily asked as she moved closer to the blue flower in front of her.

"This is the land of Naja, we are the all-seeing eye of the world," the child replied, pointing to the center of the flower. "It's the intuitive connection from the inside of Sa Neo, to the outer core."

Lily looked inside the flower. It was a dark, dark blue, almost black. And when Lily stared at the center she felt as though she was falling right through the middle of Sa Neo. Right back to the core of the world where Violetta was standing in the depth of creation. Only this time, Lily was standing amongst the flames and she could feel the fire beneath her feet too. But it wasn't burning her, she felt the energy of life, creating her. With each heartbeat it was as though an explosion of energy soared though the very core of her body and vibrate out through her veins. As she looked at the sky around, the fire appeared to be the starry galaxy, but it was confusing, for according to Lily's conscious awareness, she was viewing a combination of two worlds. The underworld and the galactic field. The inner and outer exterior had molded into one. It made absolutely no sense at all. As Lily's mind overflowed with confusion, she felt her whole body shake. It wasn't until Lily felt a tiny hand on her skin calm her, enabling her reality to shift back into place. Lily was back in the field of blue flowers, standing with the little child-like creature.

"What did you see?" the blue-haired child asked, its eyes twinkling with curiosity.

"I saw the underworld, and the outer world together as one. But I don't understand how that could be?"

"You saw the Source of creation, the energy that creates us," the child said, smiling proudly. "The two are connected. Your outer world is the repercussion of your inner world. One cannot exist without the other."

"How do you know?" Lily asked as she touched the edges of the flower.

The softness of the flower was smooth, and yet it radiated strong pulsating vibrations, as though each petal around the center held its own life, its own memory, its own thought. Yet, despite each part of the flower being completely separate, it all connected back into the center, into the middle of its source of creation.

"Because this land is the passage to our Higher Self. And through that passage we are fed the words of advice, what we call intuition. It is here that we are told the answer to any question we wish to know."

"Anything?" Lily asked as her eyes widened, and her mind immediately switched to her friends from her last visit to Sa Neo. She had already tried to see Jacques and Karisma with no such luck, the only person left was Silvia.

"Uh-huh, anything." The child winked as the stars on its forehead glistened.

"I'm looking for a small pixie fairy, her name is Silvia. Can we find her?"

"Of course! Come with me."

The small child ran through the fields of blue flowers, with only the tight bun on top of its head to show Lily the way. Lily quickly raced after it.

"Where are you?" Lily cried out loudly, as the movement of the pointy blue bun had disappeared and Lily had arrived to the edge of a thick forest.

"Up here!" shouted the small child, as its head poked down from a branch above. "You can call me Haci by the way."

"Nice to meet you, Haci, I'm Lily. Where are we going?" Lily asked as she looked around the trees. Small houses had been built amongst the branches, and there were bridges connecting each house from one to the next.

"I'm taking you to the others."

"Oh!" Lily replied, wondering what kind of creatures she would meet on this land. "I actually need to meet the Najatinis. Do you think you could take me to them?"

The small child let out a roar of laughter as it fell off the branch and onto the ground below. But as Haci touched the ground it bounced like a ball, a wobbly jelly one that rolled around. Lily jumped back, startled.

"Are you okay?" Lily asked as she rushed over to Haci.

"Yes, yes! Ah that was just too funny," Haci replied, wiping away tears of joy. "You see, you've already met one: I am a Najatini! We all are!"

And one by one, little heads appeared from the branches above, they jumped down from the trees and walked over to Lily. The Najatinis were all dressed in identical denim overalls with tight little blue buns on top of their heads. Every child had stars painted on their heads, but some had one, some had two, some had five—all were different shapes and sizes.

"Oh, wow, hello, everyone!" Lily waved as the children began to gather around her.

"This isn't everyone; come on! Follow me!" Haci said and waved its tiny hand in the air, encouraging Lily and everyone else to follow.

The tree houses were built in a long line around a great big field. There were hundreds of them! Lily felt immediately welcomed, and almost as though she was a point of interest to everyone.

"Hellotta, hellotta! We have a visitor!" Haci announced as they walked along the circumference of the field below the tree houses. As they passed each house a little Najatini popped their head out and climbed down to the ground, joining Lily and the others in a long line. Some were holding hands, others were dancing and talking amongst themselves. Lily looked behind and smiled and upon doing so, the little Najatinis would jump up and wave, with a great big smile.

By the time Lily and Haci had finished the circle, a long line of Najatinis had followed, and were now all gathering in a large crowd. Haci and Lily walked toward the middle of the field and when they reached the center, a star-shaped platform rose from the ground. Immediately all the Najatinis sat down with crossed legs around the star stage.

"Welcome fellow Najatinis! Today we are blessed with the gift of change! May I present to you, Lily," Haci announced as she pulled Lily to stand upon the stage.

The little people all nodded and giggled with one another as they hushed each other to be quiet so they could listen.

"Lily has asked a question for her third eye, and so, let's do what we do best, and show her the way!" Haci said as the crowd of Najatinis all jumped up and down and cheered.

"Now, now." Haci waved her hands to try to quieten the crowd, and immediately the Najatinis all sat back down and crossed their legs. "Lily, will you take a seat right here, it's time for you to meet your Higher Self. This is who you really are. Are you ready?" Haci asked as she encouraged Lily to take a seat in the center of the pointed star.

Lily nodded awkwardly in agreement. It wasn't that she was nervous to meet her Higher Self, she just never really knew such a connection existed. From the journey with Devya she saw that she was separate from her body, a floating Soul of energy, but now she was being told that she wasn't just a Soul, she was a higher version of her true self, one who held all the knowledge of the universe. Yet somehow when her Soul left the spirit realm and entered her body of Lily, she had forgotten everything she was told, and had to navigate through life, finding the connections, remembering the truth through the synchronizations that would fall upon her pathway.

The moment Lily sat down upon the star the most peculiar scent of crushed blueberries, cinnamon, and fennel moved through the air. As she breathed in the smell she felt a strange sensation of nurturing vibrations, as though she was being wrapped in a strong blanket of protection. And suddenly Lily could see flashes of memories push forward through her mind. Only this time, she felt as though she had remembered memories from previous lives before.

Haci had now joined the other Najatinis in the circle and together they stood up to hold hands. They all chanted in one long sound. It was a deep song that echoed through the fields of grass. The sound of the humming beat was so strong that it seemed to bring life to the air. The energy of the sound penetrated in Lily's mind, to the point that she was unable to think; all she could do was stare straight ahead, and be completely absorbed in the feelings that arose within her.

The sky around the Najatinis turned a dark blue, as though the night sky was taking over.

Haci stood up, walked over to Lily and whispered, "Place your hand on your heart and close your eyes."

Lily did as she was told. The simple placement of her hand on her heart created a nurturing, loving connection that she had never felt before. The pressure of her hand touching her skin created warmth, and a feeling of knowingness, a safe place to be herself and say anything that she needed to hear. Within seconds, a glowing light of pink-and-purple hues protruded from the center of Lily's heart. It extracted itself from Lily's body and stood in front of her. It was the most beautiful vision Lily had ever seen or felt. The ghostly light took shape, and stood before Lily, looking like a Warrior

Princess with soft pink hair that floated wildly around her face. In between the Warrior Princess's eyebrows was a slither of open space that shone brightly from within. As though the image portrayed was not real, for the light inside was the authentic truth. The Warrior Princess's eyes relaxed steadily and they gazed directly at Lily, yet when Lily looked back to her, she felt as though she moved easily between the two visions. Taking turns of being the Warrior Princess looking at herself, and then within Lily looking at the Princess. Lily gracefully floated back and forth between each angle, feeling the same awe of blissful energy that she felt when looking at the Princess, and also herself. For she was the same image, the same entity, she was a Divine Light of Angelic Energy, a Soul, who had illuminated two visions for a split moment in time to view herself as two identities, the Lily in reality, and her Higher Self.

The face of the Warrior Princess was calmly relaxed. The emotion undefined. Completely content and pleasurably relaxed. As Lily opened her mind up to the idea that her Soul was not only in her body but also a higher extension of her authentic self, the Warrior Princess moved closer to her, and molded inside Lily once more. Only this time, she spoke through Lily, and it was the sound of Lily's own voice inside her head, her heart, and vibrating through the entire space of reality around them.

"I'm here with you always, Lily," the voice said. "You are so deeply loved. You were born for a reason. You are living for a purpose. You are here to create and accomplish great things. Everything is going to be okay."

A single tear formed in the corner of Lily's right eye as the words she so longed to hear from someone were being told to herself, from herself. Yet even though she had searched everywhere for someone else to reassure her, she was the one who was saying these words to provide a feeling of comfort that had never been felt. As the tear released from her eye down her cheek, it was as though all the built-up angst and worry of uncertainty in her life was shed too. That single tear was an extraction from her body that encompassed a great deal more than she could ever understand. It held all the confusion of who she was and why she was born to live a life. It carried all the pain of not knowing, all the questions, the misunderstandings, and she let it go. Not because the questions were answered, but because she didn't need to know. For her Higher Self had all the answers, and was delivering her the right messages, she was protected always, and therefore, she just needed to surrender to the life around her as she walked hand in hand in alignment with her Higher Self. Even though she didn't know the way, she knew she was being guided, and that to her was more important than anything else.

"I want to speak to you more often," Lily whispered through her mind.

"I am always here. Place your hand on your heart anytime you want to talk," she heard the voice of herself whisper back.

The sound of a loud gong echoed through the park, and the chanting stopped. The Warrior Princess returned into the center of Lily's heart, and Lily felt herself come back into reality. She exhaled in a great sigh, feeling an overload of emotions and buzzing energy circulate through her body.

"That was ...absolutely incredible!" Lily said as she finally regained consciousness. "I never knew I was so magical. And so, the Higher Self, our Soul, resides inside our heart?"

"Your Soul is everywhere. It's not limited to the parameters of your body. It is an energy field that derives from the center of your heart but it is tall and wide well past the exterior," Haci said as it walked up to Lily and touched her hand. "This is also why you must be careful when being too close to other people's energy; it is easy to absorb those who you do not wish to absorb."

Lily nodded as she recalled feeling ill one evening after spending too much time sitting next to a girl in her class who she didn't like very much. And it was so strange, she remembered, it wasn't the normal feeling of ill, just a strange mental feeling of exhaustion. As though something was sucking her energy out and replacing it with something horrific. *It all made sense,* she thought.

"But I forgot to ask where Silvia was." Lily looked at Haci alarmed, annoyed at herself for forgetting the original task. It was as though everything else around her disappeared when she channeled her Higher Self. Like nothing mattered, everything was peaceful, and everything was calm as is.

"You know the answer to everything. Here, tap into your Higher Self with me. Place your hand on your heart and ask your Higher Self where Silvia is ..."

Lily mirrored Haci's action and closed her eyes. The sound of one word came through her heart; it was the name of the land, Salor.

"Salor," Lily recited.

"Wonderful!" Haci replied, clapping her hands gleefully once more.

Lily smiled as she stood up, but she quickly sat back down again, feeling as though her legs were unable to carry her.

"I feel uneasy," Lily said as she lay down on the ground, breathing slowly.

"That's okay, you just bypassed the logic of time and space," Haci said as it pulled out a small frankincense stick and burned it. "Here, this will help."

And with one hand it twirled the burning wood around Lily, soothing her with the smell, and tickling her senses all at once.

"Hema ou era wiy," Haci chanted, as it blew the smoke gently over Lily and then turned to the crowd and repeated the action. "The smoke is allowing safe passageway of the light energy back to you," Haci continued.

"That really was so wonderful!" Lily exclaimed, now finally feeling herself. "I wish more people could feel that divine love of connection and support."

"Everyone can, they just choose not to." Haci chuckled as it helped Lily to stand up again.

As Lily stood up an idea jumped through her mind too, as though the voice of her intuition was speaking through to her loudly.

"That's it!" Lily shrieked. "That's how we can ignite the revolution. By teaching the people of Praza how to connect to their Higher Self!" Lily continued as she felt strength in her own voice. "I know you cannot get involved in the war, but this is just passing wisdom, this could be allowed, right?"

Lily was too excited to wait for the answer and her eyes opened wide, desperately waiting for a response. Haci looked to the other Najatinis, who all whispered together and huddled amongst themselves.

"We've come to an agreement," announced Haci as it turned toward Lily. "We would be honored!"

"Hooray!" Lily squealed with a huge smile of relief. "This might be the answer to everything! Because if the people of Praza loved themselves more, and felt this self-acceptance, they wouldn't feel the need to obey another's orders, for they would know they have the power within themselves."

"Well, we can certainly try!" Haci replied, as all the Najatinis smiled and nodded in the crowd.

"But first, I believe I should try to see Silvia. I cannot leave Sa Neo without knowing if she is safe. Would it be okay to please meet in Praza? Perhaps at sunrise tomorrow? We could meet at the big fountain in the middle of the village?"

"Yes!" The Najatinis all nodded their heads quickly, gleefully bouncing up and down upon the ground like little rubber balls.

Lily thanked the Najatinis dearly and hugged them all goodbye, leaving the land of Naja with an overwhelming sense of happiness. She felt as though she had ticked all the boxes of achievements. She had confronted her past, truly acknowledged the core of the problem, and forgiven herself. This then had now opened up the space to allow something new to enter, and she felt as though this new energy had already come through to her from her wonderful idea. The realization she had through the connection with her Higher Self was something Lily would take with her all her life, and she vowed to share the wisdom with everyone that she could. For she now knew that this was the secret to living an honest life, an authentic life, it was just the answer she needed to lead and encourage others to see the beauty within themselves. She had discovered how to save the world, and the solution was by simply honoring the loving light within.

nineteen

The Land of Salor

Lily arrived to the yellow-crystal land of Salor as the sun was shining brightly in the sky. It radiated a strong heat, much hotter than any of the other lands she had ever felt. Even the crystals beneath her feet felt too hot to touch, and she jumped up and down hurriedly, running off the beach onto the closest landing. But the closest base that Lily could find was a charcoal stump of a tree that had burned down. As Lily looked around the land, she could see that the majority of the trees had burned down too, leaving a smell of smoke that lingered in the air. The sound of animals and wildlife was nowhere to be heard from the lack of shelter and weight of crushing heat. Lily jumped to the next tree stump surrounded with ashes, and the next one after that. She wasn't sure where to walk, but a path of fine crystals shining brightly in the distance seemed to attract Lily's attention. Although from the desert heat it could've been a mirage.

Still, Lily didn't question the sign and continued toward the path, and as she did so, small cacti began to pop up along it, encouraging Lily to follow. After several minutes, Lily eventually made her way to a great golden arch created out of clay. The top of the arch opened up wide, blocking the sun out yet allowing a wind to flow through. Lily could see through the archway, and into the other side of the opening; however, it didn't appear to be any different from where she was standing. But when Lily walked through it she didn't come out the other side, she had magically arrived into the village of Salor, so different from before; she felt as though she had walked into a completely different land. The temperature was much cooler, and lush green gardens now took over the desert land, with pools of shallow water. Many village folk were playing in the water, swimming and splashing merrily. No one seemed to notice Lily's presence at all.

Lily walked up to an old lady sitting on a large stone that was carved out as though it were a long chair. She sat very peacefully watching the children splash in the water. Lily could feel how much the lady loved it and she wondered what memories played through her head, or what her thoughts were. Even though Lily wanted to know where her dear friend Silvia was, she felt a strong urge to connect with the old lady, and she promptly sat down next to her.

"Hello," Lily said as she sat on the park bench near the old lady.

The lady gazed in Lily's direction and nodded lightly.

"Hello," she said, smiling.

As she spoke her eyes glistened, a soft vibration of changing colors. She moved slowly as she spoke to Lily, her head and body shaking slightly as the words vibrated from her body.

"Are you from Salor?" Lily asked, realizing that perhaps she might know where Silvia lived.

"I'm from everywhere." The old lady smiled, moving a little bit closer to Lily. "I've seen the world change a great deal. The evolution of people, of villages."

Her voice trailed off as she looked to the side, as though reliving her life in a photographic memoir.

"How splendid," Lily replied, now realizing there was much to be learned. "And where do you live now? Is this your home?"

"Home. It's a beautiful word, isn't it?" she replied, running her finger over the corner of the chair that she was sitting on. "It's not a place, but a feeling, really. I felt it in the land upon where I was born. Although, I left that world a long time ago. I did what I needed to do."

The old lady winked at Lily, implying that she knew what she was talking about.

"What did you need to do?"

"Explore the galaxies and meet new faces. I connected with many people. I exchanged energy with creatures of all kinds. That was my purpose. And now, we are here to meet together too."

Lily nodded with admiration. There was something strangely enchanting about the old lady.

"Why do you think we are to meet today?" Lily asked, finding herself as well touching the edge of the chair, feeling the tip of the stone smooth and sharp.

"To talk about the revolution. I am the one who ignited the change for generations to come. It is because of me that the people remembered the power they held inside," the lady replied, opening her eyes wide. They now resembled a dark green, with splinters of black, and her hair changed into dark curls, messy curls. As Lily looked into the old lady's eyes she felt a strange sense of familiarity, and slowly in front of Lily, magically, the years of age began to disappear from her face and body. She transformed from an old woman into a mother, into an adult, into a teenager, and then into the face of Lily.

Lily held her breath, but it didn't last long, for the replicate of Lily changed into a child, and then a baby, and then—nothing. There was nothing in front of Lily. No children playing around her. Lily was sitting on the bench all by herself, as the sun rose high in the sky, completely alone, on the land of Salor.

twenty

The Truth

The breeze in the air grew thicker, and with it drifted the sound of a child's voice, a high-pitched lullaby that weaved through the trees like the web of a spider's thread. The song clung to everything that it passed, cocooning it with love. The voice was unmistakable: it was the sound of her friend, Silvia. Lily followed the voice through the village, as though being pulled along a string of energy. The song wrapped around her body like a long scarf and before she knew it, she was standing in front of the door of a quaint little cottage.

Knock, knock, knock.

As Lily rapped her knuckles to the wooden door, she felt a surplus of nervous energy pulsating through her body. It was the excitement from seeing someone that she hadn't seen for a very long time, and a hint of fear, wondering if Silvia would remember her or not.

"Hello ..." came Silvia's voice as she opened the door, revealing a much older fairy, still as beautiful as ever, with long silver hair and pointy slippers.

"Silvia?" Lily asked as she smiled and held her arms out wide nervously.

"Lily?" Silvia opened her tiny mouth and blinked three times, her silver eyelashes flickering, unsure if she was actually dreaming.

"Yes! It's me!" Lily said as she rushed forward and hugged the fairy, feeling her little arms around her.

"I never thought you'd come back," Silvia whispered, her cheeks exploding in a shade of red roses.

"I've always thought about you." Lily smiled, now holding Silvia's hands. "I'm so happy to see that you escaped!"

"I've always thought about you too," Silvia replied, and she half smiled, as though feeling unworthy of her freedom.

Silvia looked deeply into Lily's eyes, and as she did, Lily felt that deep sorrow of the years stolen from her when she was a slave to Jade. Even though she had left that life, the scars from her past were engraved in her memory, constantly reminding her of what happened.

"Please do come in." Silvia said as she opened the door wide, encouraging Lily to walk through.

The moment Lily entered the space she felt as though she had just walked into a room that expressed the beautiful inner being of Silvia, the one that she had been forced to hide for so long. The walls were covered entirely in an assortment of yellow flowers: sunflowers, roses, tulips, daffodils, dahlias, peonies, and every kind of flower that could be imagined, painted in yellow. Then, of course, there were the unusual flowers that Lily had never seen before. Ones with diamond-pointed petals and huge flowers with hundreds of tiny circles around it. The whole room smelled of a lovely garden.

"Oh, wow, Silvia, your home is absolutely beautiful."

"Thank you," Silvia gushed, nodding her head lightly as she shyly looked at the yellow flowers on the walls. "I always thought this is what I'd create if I was ever to survive." She looked at Lily and smiled. "Here, let me show you around. This is where I sleep," Silvia continued as she pointed to a pile of lush yellow pillows in the far corner. "And, over here, I meditate every day," she said as she pointed to a large circular rug with a flower print that stemmed from the inside out. "And my kitchen is through there." She pointed to a small circular opening with no door in the opposite corner.

"Silvia, this is beautiful! You have created the life that you always wanted to, I'm so happy for you," Lily said as she looked around the house seeing Silvia's personality shown everywhere. "May I ask …if it doesn't bring up sad memories, but, oh, however did you escape?"

Silvia nodded gravely as though she knew the time had come to tell the story. "Come, let's have some tea and cake and I will tell you."

Silvia poured hot tea into the small golden-painted cups, and the smell of crushed chamomile wafted through the air. Lily took a bite of Plum Kisses cakes that Silvia had made. They melted in her mouth like almond butter, soft and delectable. She enjoyed it thoroughly. But several minutes had now passed and Silvia still had not spoken. Lily looked to Silvia patiently waiting for her friend to tell her.

Silvia took a sip of tea, brushed her silver hair back again from her face and looked out through the window as she pondered on her thoughts. The wind blew through the trees as that moment, and it howled with great strength.

"The weather has changed as a result of all this war, did you notice?"

Silvia was right, Lily thought as she remembered how different the energy of the air felt. But she had thought that it was just natural changes. And then Lily remembered the time she went underwater with the mermaids on her last visit, and how she danced around the great ball of Neo, the beautiful flaming fire in the center of the ocean. How it had made the volcanoes erupt with great strength the next day. She had wondered how interconnected the underwater world was to the upper land. How the cycle of death was being repeated or rejected through the weather. A tangible creation that would never be controlled by anyone. And yet it suffered from the repercussions of their actions, from the killing of the mermaids.

"After you left, and the mermaids left, the lands began to change. The weather grew fierce, it would either be too hot or unbearably cold. The waterfall stopped moving, or it would flood for days at a time. The world changed, and not for the better." Silvia shivered as she began the story, and she placed her teacup on the short golden table.

"Jade's temper became extremely volatile," Silvia continued. "One day she would demand ridiculous commands, and another, she would sleep all day, never leaving her bed or speaking to anyone. She was drunk with power, wanting to make sure that everyone feared her. But we had had enough. We knew we were being manipulated. We wanted our life back. We wanted our freedom. We couldn't go on being a slave to her ruling. To a ruling that made no sense for the people. That didn't help us in any way." Silvia's emotion now grew to anger as she stepped back inside the memory of what once was.

"She wouldn't let me leave, Lily. I knew where my family was; I had to come back here, but she wouldn't let me leave." Silvia's tears began to surface as she remembered the story. "She started to hurt the old man who played the ukulele. She said he wasn't allowed to eat if he didn't walk along a painted line. But, Lily, he's very old. His eyesight is poor. Only a child could walk that line, not an old man. It was awful Lily, simply awful. She made fun of him and laughed and forced all of us to laugh. And that night, I just couldn't bear it. I didn't want to be told what to do anymore. Of living a life according to someone else's reign. And why? Why did I have to live for someone else's pleasure? When she wasn't doing anything to help another. She wasn't doing anything to support the lives of those around her."

Silvia hopped off her cushion and began pacing around the room. She screwed up her small fists in the air as a surplus of emotion shook through her little body vigorously. "There had been rumors about the magical power of the Ikinu plant. The Ikinu was a tiny herb no bigger than the size of a grain of salt, and it had been rumored that if one was to swallow this plant it would put them into a deep sleep. We all organized it. One night, the others covered for me, and I went deep into the forest to find it." Silvia crouched down to Lily, as she whispered the truth.

"I crept into the shadows near the Sacred Valley of Lucidity, and it was here that I stole the blood from the Ikinu Tree. The sap screamed as it bled from the roots, and I poured it into a tiny glass bottle, and delivered it safely to the cook. When Jade drank the tea, she died in an instant. All the servants were free." Silvia smiled, remembering the great rejoice of their victory. "But the news of what had happened didn't come out in the truth. Well, I heard this is what happened in the land of Praza. The only story they know is that the mermaids were captured, and that Jade is dead."

Silvia sighed and rested back in her chair. She was exhausted having felt such strong emotions downpour through her small frame, and she looked back to Lily, worried.

"Is it justice what I did, Miss Lily? Or do you think the God of Karma will come and serve its hand?"

Lily looked to the small teacup in her hand, and at the hot water inside. She breathed in the smell of chamomile, unsure how to explain her thoughts. Yet, at the same time, Lily wasn't sure what her thoughts were. Whether she supported or condemned the matter.

"I think that you need to make peace with yourself and come forward to explain what it is that you did. The role you played in setting yourself free. Allow the repercussions of what has been done to play out. They will play out, regardless of your meddling in them," Lily replied, although she was unsure where her point of view came from. For the very question that Silvia was asking—for forgiveness—was what Lily had been seeking all along.

"You always say the right things, Miss Lily." Silvia nodded with approval. "Here, I want to show you something," Silvia said as she took Lily to a stairwell to the left of the door.

Together they walked up a few windy steps until they reached an attic at the top. And there in front of Lily was a heavenly decorated bath tub. It was a long, rectangular bath that sat in the middle of the room with large glass walls and ceilings all around.

"This is my favorite place, I made it in honor of you," Silvia said as she smiled admiringly with her yellow eyes, and she displayed a large table full of luscious bath products.

"Me? How? And you don't have to call me Miss Lily anymore. Remember? Lily is fine." Lily giggled as she hovered over the small jars of sweet-smelling herbs and oils of lavender and rosemary.

"Sorry, old habits." Silvia nodded. "You inspired me to create this bath because ...well ..." And it was here that Silvia shied away. But not from fear, she had tears in her eyes. "I created it in honor for what you did for me. I've never forgotten, Lily. You gave me courage and strength when I had none. I thought that my life could never be changed. But you gave me hope. You stood up for what you believed in and you encouraged me to do the same." Silvia smiled, wiping away small tears of joy. "Most of our time together was spent when I would draw you a bath, remember?"

"Yes, of course I remember." Lily smiled, remembering that even though her time in Jade's castle was unusually disturbing, the sanctuary she found while lying in the bath was rejuvenating and nurturing. Like a big, warm hug.

"Well, I never told you this, but, you always seemed so different after your bath time. Like, you were more ...I don't know how to say it. But you were more yourself. You stood with grace and confidence. It was like the water had washed away any problems you had encountered during the day and you appeared to be stronger from within," Silvia said as she brushed her hair back from her face. "And so, this bath is in honor of our time together, in memory of you, and it's a way to remind me of who I really am and where I came from."

"Silvia, it's me who is truly honored, thank you," Lily replied, feeling an overflow of warmth move through her body from the kindness of her friend's words. "I had no idea how different I was after a bath, but you're right now that I think about it, I felt more harmoniously balanced. How funny what just a simple bath can do! If only Jade took a bath, imagine how different her rules might have been!" Lily joked, wishing evil could be cleansed from a little bit of water.

"Oh, Miss Lily, but she was a different person after her bath too. Only a few got to see it though. I guess because they were the only times she was able to show her true self. None of her fancy clothes, or that painted face. Without any makeup she could finally let that ugly tattoo on her face breathe, and perhaps she felt better knowing she was owning up to herself."

Lily felt like a pin had just pricked her skin, and all the hairs on her body shot out straight at once.

"What do you mean that Jade had a tattoo on her face?"

"Yes, oh, you never saw it? It's a universal stain, like a karmic equality. If you steal children from other lands your face would automatically create a tattoo. I thought you knew. It's kind of like a branding, to warn others."

Lily felt a freezing cold shiver smack her body. The kind of feeling she used to get when she'd jump into the ocean early in the morning before the sun had warmed the seas up. Only, instead of adjusting to the temperature, the shadow of cold lingered, and it ran up and down like shooting needles all over her body. It crept up high into her head, freezing her mind for several seconds as a splitting headache took control.

"Miss Lily, are you okay? You look white," Silvia asked, worried, and she put her hand on Lily's. "You're freezing!" Silvia said as she covered Lily's shoulders with a shawl.

Lily blinked for several seconds as an explosion of thoughts swam through her mind. And the flashbacks of everyone around her that she had seen. The tattoo-faced girl in Karisma's home, the tattoo-faced lady in the fountain place, and, worst of all, Marlina! Lily replayed the memories over in her head but this time as she recalled her encounters with Marlina, she remembered the faces of the children. The eeriness of their smiles, and the way they spoke their words. But one thing Lily couldn't understand was why would she pretend to be on Lily's side and go against her own people? The thoughts kept racing around Lily's mind for several minutes, and it wasn't until Silvia had opened a pouch of coffee beans and placed them under Lily's nose to wake her up that she finally came through.

"Oh, Silvia, I'm sorry. I didn't mean to worry you. It's just ..." Lily lost her words, she was praying that she didn't hear Silvia right, wondering if she had dreamed of something strange. "It's just because of what you had said, about the tattoo-faced people. So they are the ones who steal children from other lands? They aren't good people?"

Lily stared at Silvia in the eyes, desperate for it not to be true.

"If someone has a tattoo on their face, it's because they have stolen a child, one or many. And that child has been sold on, or used for their own amusement. They are the worst kind of people in the world."

"How do you know?"

"Because of my father. The day he sold me to Jade's people, a tattoo appeared on his face. It was so terribly ghastly that it was then he realized what he had done, but it was too late."

"Where is he now?" Lily asked, wondering how difficult it must be to live knowing that her own parent betrayed her trust. And Lily realized how lucky she was to have a father who loved her, and even though her mother had passed away, she loved her just as much.

"I never saw him again. He left to travel the world with his new-found riches. He only received wisdom of magic in return, that was all he wanted. He sold me for his own greed. All I know is that he has a dotted-line tattoo near his ear."

The image of Arra popped into Lily's head with his yellow eyes, and the tattoo scar near his ear.

"If you could see him, do you think you would want to?"

Silvia looked at Lily sternly in the eye. It was the first time she didn't cower, or turn her head down shyly. It was as though she had anticipated that situation for many, many years.

"I want to see him and tell him that I forgive him. I send him love, and I hope he is safe every day."

"Even though he did what he did?"

"The thing is, I know why he did it. My mother explained that his father lost all his magic as he grew older with age. One day, his father awoke with an inability to perform witchcraft, and so my father was terrified to become like him. So I understand it wasn't his doing, it was the knock-on effect from his father. I want to tell him I forgive him. I want to repair our relationship."

"Silvia, I think I met him. I traveled to Neveah when I first arrived to find Violetta, and I met a short man named ..." But the memory of the man had disappeared from Lily's mind. "The same name forward and backward, it was ..."

"Arra?"

"Yes!"

"Oh, Lily, you've given me two gifts now. You really are a blessing to this world. You're connecting people and places together without even realizing it." Silvia said with a warm smile as she nodded proudly and walked with Lily back down the stairwell and into the lounge area.

"Silvia, that's it! That's how we heal completely—through forgiveness. We need to forgive those who hurt us, we need to forgive the ancestors who have passed. The healing isn't just for this lifetime, we need to clear thousands of years of conditioning, and send love and more love to the ancestors who have passed, so that their hurt, blame, and pain doesn't continue and pollute the next generation. And into the lives of the children that follow."

The image of the Najatinis flashed into Lily's eyes and the promise she had made to meet them on Praza. *But why the Najatinis?* Lily wondered, as she recalled Marlina's suggestion to bring them. *They were the all-seeing eye of the world, the connection to the Higher Self. If Marlina and the tattoo-faced people were able to control this element of the world, they would dominate it.*

"Oh Silvia. I'm sorry, I can't stay any longer. I've just realized the truth. I must go and stop the Najatinis from coming to Praza, I think I've just walked them into their own trap!" Lily jumped up quickly, shaking her head. "Oh, if evil took complete control of the world's intuition they would have ultimate power. I must stop it, I must!" Lily shrieked as she picked up her belongings and rushed to give Silvia a hug. "Silvia, thank you for everything, truly. I will visit you again soon, I promise!"

Silvia hugged Lily tightly in response and nodded with understanding. Lily took out her orange crystals and walked to the closest tree for shelter. She took a deep breath, closed her eyes and cleared her mind, calming it down, despite the rage she felt within. And as she tedimeta'd to Praza, she repeated the same prayer over and over in her mind, "Najatini's do not help! Stay in Naja!"

twenty-one

Death Moon

Lily arrived on the beach of Praza as the sun rose high in the sky. She looked up at the trees that lined the beach, but they felt different now. Lily felt as though she could see the veins of the trees vibrate in a loud heartbeat. She walked close to one and hugged it tightly and sure enough, she felt as though the vibrating pulses of the underworld were moving through her. Lily's own heart began to beat a deep, rhythmic sound in alignment with the liveliness of the trees that surrounded her. With each strumming beat Lily felt like she could hear some words come through to her: they were saying, "Do not fear. All is meant to be."

She walked toward the village, but no one was awake, it was completely quiet. Luckily, the Najatinis were nowhere to be seen, and Lily wondered if in fact her prayers had been heard. *But, surely the Najatini's were too wise to know if they were being misled,* Lily reasoned in her mind. And then there was a glimpse of hope lingering in Lily's thoughts, that perhaps Marlina really did want to change, and she knew the way to let go of her evil ways was to get in touch with her Higher Self.

Lily continued to walk through the town until she reached the Marlina Residence. She hovered outside for several minutes, contemplating what to do. Behind the door was a lie and at the same time, there were children who needed to be saved. A part of her wanted to slam the door down and expose Marlina for who she really was, and the other part was terrified to face the corruption. But either way she chose to go, she knew she needed to be clever to succeed, and careful. She had to pretend like she knew no different to before, and act as though Marlina was on her side. So with a deep breath, and a brave face, Lily knocked on the door.

"You came back," Airlie said as she opened the door and rushed to give Lily a hug. "I've missed you," Airlie continued, looking up with her beautiful orange eyes. The outer circle around her iris twinkled lightly, and it swirled around with a dancing gleam.

"I've missed you too," Lily replied, forcing a smile on her face as she followed Airlie into the room to join the others. It wasn't difficult for Lily to smile, but it was hard to swallow the tears from knowing that Airlie was held against her will.

Marlina was polishing silver ornaments, and Oceana and Leafy were playing a board game together with small brass figurines. Lily could now feel the stale energy as she entered the room. The children all sat up straight, with a weird smile again, as though they were being controlled.

"Lily!" Marlina said joyously. "So, you've finally returned. And is today the day?" Marlina asked, as she picked up the next silver ornament on the kitchen shelf. It was a small sculpture of a tiger, and the tail moved side to side as Marlina rubbed the edges of it.

"Ah ...yes, I believe so," Lily replied uneasily, as she played with her amethyst ring, trying to move her attention elsewhere.

"Did you find the Najatinis? Are they coming?" Marlina asked, lowering her gaze, and she tilted her head slightly, her ear aching to hear Lily's answer.

"Yes," Lily replied as she looked back to Marlina, knowing that she needed to appear confident if she was to pretend everything was okay.

The family stood in silence for several seconds. No one moved.

"But first, I wish to speak to the village people, can I?" Lily continued, although she was unsure where the voice had come from.

"Of course. We've been waiting for this for a very long time," Marlina replied as she took the hands of the children and stood in front of Lily. "Shall we?"

Lily turned and walked back along the hallway and out the front door with Marlina and the children following. In the short amount of time that Lily had been inside, the village was now buzzing. People were walking around, dancing, and singing. Lily walked up to the center of the fountain where the village folk were gathering water. She felt nervous, but the confidence of knowing that she was doing the right thing overtook her rationality and took a deep breath, reminding herself that everything was going to be okay.

Next, Lily picked up a long wooden stick, and drew a large circle with it. As she drew, she used her free hand to feel the energy vibrations alongside it. The words from Devya sifted through her mind as she moved her hand, and in a loud voice Lily said, "This is my sacred space. Come forth everyone and unite with me."

The sound from Lily's words moved through the air, floating like a soft purring drum as the village folk walked closer toward her. For a moment, Lily didn't want to go through with it. She felt very hot, and her clothes felt sticky, like they didn't belong to her. Her voice sounded a little squeaky, as though she didn't believe in herself. She wanted the easy option out. But deep inside she knew that to stand up for what she believed in was the easy option, for if she didn't, she would have to live every day knowing that she could've helped another but she chose not to. And so she cleared her throat, took another deep breath, and commenced.

"Fellow friends in Praza, I have gathered you here today to ignite a change, to create a better future," Lily said as the crowd started to fill out. She looked around at the innocent faces, and even though only half were showing their support, Lily could sense the other half were curious. "It begins from an idea of what it'd be like to live in peace. A world where it's safe to express ourselves freely. It is a place where all are accepted despite our ancestral history. There is great knowledge to be learned from one another, and we are being foolish not to listen. We're stopping the lineage of wisdom from lifetimes before, when their voices need to be heard. For they hold the answer to your prayers. The way to peace is through unity, and it can only be achieved if we break down the barriers that separate us, and hold our hands out to help each other," Lily continued as the words flowed through her body effortlessly. It was as though she had reached down within her heart, and nurtured her Soul as she asked for support, but instead, her Soul had taken over, speaking the words of truth through her chest and into the crowd around her.

"I came here to save you, but in truth, only you can save yourself. You are strong enough to stand on your own, you just need to believe it. It's time to take your power back, but before you do, you need to find where you lost it in the first place. When was it in your life that you believed that you were unworthy of love? When did you start to fear the power of your own self? Why are you giving your power away to a leader who doesn't want equality? We cannot follow someone who does not wish for peace amongst the lands. From this moment onwards I ask that you take back your power. I ask that you say no to the slaughtering of innocent creatures. Let us abide by the rules of creation and reward the lands that have gifted us everything!" Lily's body was shaking with energy as the words burst through her chest and into the air around her.

She felt as though they floated above the crowd, seeping slowly into their ears and through their entities. It only took a few smiles from the crowd to let Lily know that she was on the right path, and with determination she continued. "We need to remember where we came from," she said as she pointed to beneath the ground, remembering Violetta creating the babies from the natural resources of the world, the combination of energy and matter erupting together as one. "We chose these bodies, we chose this land to live upon. What is it that you think you are here to do? Imagine the kind of world we could create if we were to combine our powers together? If we learned from each other, from both the people of the land and the creatures in the sea, just imagine the kind of magic that could potentially exist. What if ...what if ...what if we changed the world for lifetimes to come? I ask you now. Place your hand on your heart and tell me what it says." Lily opened the palm of her hand and placed it on her heart, as half of the crowd mirrored her action. "Can you live a life being the best version of yourself that you can possibly be? It's time for us to make a change. We can do it. There is power in our numbers and we cannot do this alone, but we can do it together. Who's with me?"

A thunderous applause echoed through the village, as those who supported Lily stomped on the ground and clapped their hands in the air. But it was still only half of the crowd that agreed with Lily's words, and the other half looked angrily at her. A tall fat man pushed through to the front and he entered Lily's circle, standing next to her in her sacred space.

"We don't know this girl!" the fat man yelled out, as the those who were against Lily cheered him on. "Who is she to tell us what to do?"

"Yes, you're right. It's true." Lily nodded in agreement. "You don't know me. But I know you. I am that foreign girl that Allura told you about. I know the truth of what happened to Jade. It's because of my visit to this world that Jade died."

The crowd looked at each other shocked with the unexpected news. But Lily didn't feel like a threat, she finally felt like she was able to share her story and put it down to rest. She looked to the fat man who was now speechless, unsure of what to do, and so Lily continued.

"When I first came to Sa Neo, a long time ago, I was seeking clarity in my life. I was searching for the answers to my problems. And I did, I solved many puzzles within myself, I managed to soothe so much of the conflicting pain within my heart, but while doing so, I unraveled deeper truths, and entwined pasts. It is me who brought forward the mermaids and connected them to this world. It was because of me that they were found out after living many years in peace. But this is where you have it wrong, they are good creatures, not your toys. They are playful and curious, and full of wild magic that we can only try to understand. Their magic is not yours to steal." Lily said as she recalled the incredible power that lived on beneath the ocean.

"I was terrified to come back here, unsure of what I would find. But in truth, I found myself. I had been denying what had happened. I locked away the hurt I felt inside myself, throwing my pain away into a tiny part inside of me, but I need to let it breathe, because it's a big part of me, one that doesn't need to define me, but that helps mold me into the person I am today. So today, I ask you. If you are looking for forgiveness. Forgive yourself. If you want to change the life you are leading, then do it. To the tattoo-faced people you can be free. It's never too late to change. But you need to set yourself free, own up to your mistakes and stop passing the blame. Is this evil in your heart because of you or because of your ancestors? If it's the latter, let's journey together to forgive them and send them love. We are all doing the best we know how to. We are all just trying out hardest to be heard, to seek validation and comfort and love."

Lily raised her hands up high as though feeling the energy of love that floating in the air, and in return the sound of musical drums and flutes began to play, in support of her words, in gratitude for Lily sharing her story. Lily looked around to find the children and Marlina, but neither were in sight, for the crowd was too busy dancing and singing. But the sounds of joy did not last very long. For a great bang of lightning burst through the air, and an eruption of orange smoke blasted in the center of the village. When the smoke finally cleared, there before the crowd stood Queen Allura.

Allura looked more beautiful than she ever looked before. Her hair was pulled back tightly, showcasing the shape of her face—a strong jawline and darting eyes. The arrangement of her eyebrows, nose, and lips were beyond perfection. Luscious lips with large features, it was a dominating force. She wore a long skirt full of tiny mirrors which reflected her surroundings like a shining light. The same mirrors were cut out over her chest, but placed as though stuck to her skin, in a shadow of clusters. Her diamond crown weighed heavily on her forehead. Each mirror reflected off the other and the diamonds shot sparkling lights into the air in all directions.

"So, you have returned to my land, I see," Allura said as she placed her hands on her hips fiercely, and stared directly at Lily, her pupils blazing with orange fire inside.

But Lily felt strong in her stance and she stood up tall, balancing her shoulders and rising her neck.

"I have come to tell the true story," Lily said, as opened her arms to the crowd.

"The true story?" Allura laughed, a great, deep snickering that felt more like a wailing sound from a wild beast.

Allura felt no fear and she showed it bravely. She was confident in her powers, and perhaps that was the greatest secret of them all. For it allowed her to prey off the weak by instantly dismissing their attempt to threaten.

"I am here to tell the people from Praza the truth about what happened to Jade. You cannot rewrite the history any longer." Lily said as she cleared her throat and stared at Allura, counteracting her intimidation. It was in that moment that Lily felt as though she was taller than anyone else around her. As though her words were flowing with great energy behind them. "Allura has been telling you lies," Lily continued, as the crowd hushed down to listen. And they looked to one another curiously, wondering who to believe. "Jade was killed by her own people."

"Lies!" Allura yelled back as she pointed to Lily, instructing the soldiers of Allura to march over to where Lily was standing, but the crowd was too thick, and they could not get through.

"She treated the people the same way you are being treated now, feeding them lies to keep them in fear, to make them believe that they needed her. But the people woke up, and they knew it was wrong. Jade stole creatures from other lands, and she tricked them by making them believe they were unworthy; they did not realize their own power. Allura wants to keep you small so that you obey her. But it doesn't have to be this way. You have great strength amongst you. You are wise, you are intelligent, and you are meant to live freely."

"Take her!" Allura yelled again, but instead of the soldiers, this time a group of women and men with the tattoos on their faces leapt from the crowd toward her. But Lily was smarter than before, and she quickly envisioned a protective bubble around her being. She saw the light from high above, it moved quickly past the sky, from the stars in the universe; they shone down brightly upon her, and they carved a deep bubble around her body, sheltering her from another coming in.

Allura's face changed color to a dark orange, and she let out a great scream, as she pointed to a large cloud above and pulled it over Lily, squashing the protective bubble from moving. Lily was now stuck in between the land and the sky.

"Ugh, you can never rely on anyone other than yourself." Allura laughed as she threw her hand up, pleased with her own actions. "Now, enough playtime. Where are the Najatinis?" Allura asked loudly as she scanned the faces of the villagers.

"They are coming soon," came a voice from within the crowd.

"Who said that? Come forward," Allura commanded, as the crowd parted, and there stood Marlina, holding the hands of the three children.

Marlina now appeared completely different to how Lily had seen her before. Her clothes were much more elegant. She was draped in thick orange silk, with fine sparkling circles and tiny seeds sewn along the trimming. The children looked more weary than before, wearing raggedy clothes, with dirty faces. They looked like street beggars, searching for leftover food. The perfect image that Lily once saw had disappeared, and the glimpse of truth that had once revealed itself to her every so often was finally free.

"Very good." Allura smiled at Marlina, and with her free hand she threw her finger toward the closest servant, who quickly ran and gifted Marlina a grand orange crystal necklace.

Marlina's eyes opened wide in admiration and she gasped with a devilish squeal as she put the necklace on.

"Oh, it's beautiful, thank you."

"I always reward my subjects," Allura said as she winked, and then she pointed her finger back to Lily. "Now, as for you. Why don't you tell the people the truth? Someone saw you." Allura raised her eyebrows, as she put her hands on her hips and stood up tall. "Where is my friend, my loyal friend?"

Allura moved her head looking for someone, and as she did so, the reflection of the sun shone onto the mirrored dress, spraying heat to those around her. "Ah! There you are. Come and tell us what you saw!"

Allura was talking to one of the fishermen. He rolled forward with a wobbly belly and a feather-stuffed hat, but instead of talking, he opened up his palm, waiting to be rewarded first. Allura once again gave the signal, and this time the man received a large potion, to which he chugged down quickly and loudly. Lily couldn't help but think how repulsive his manners were.

"He's busy." Allura smirked and rolled her eyes mockingly. "He told me that you shape-shifted into a mermaid." Allura laughed with anger, and she spat on the ground where Lily stood. "You are one of them. You are a degenerate to our race. And now, you will be our new sacrifice to the Gods so that we may travel together to the afterworld. There will be enough for everyone!"

The other half of the crowd who had been silent during Lily's speech now cheered with happiness, as though desperate to journey to the afterlife with Allura. It was evident that they too had become addicted to the riches of Allura. If they weren't gifted with jewels, or potions, they were rewarded through an experience, and that was worthy enough to trade the life of another.

But Lily wasn't scared. And instead, she placed her hand on her heart again, encouraging the crowd to do the same. To which they did. Lily felt loving energy circle around her hand and the contact of skin to skin provided her with nurturing support once again. As the village folk around Lily mimicked her actions, small sparkles of rainbow lights lifted through everyone's fingertips and shot up high above. They exploded above their heads like fireworks in the night sky. Lily smiled, knowing she had the support of the crowd around her. But Allura growled in response, pulling her lips behind her teeth and frowning her brows with strength. Her eyes were orange and watery, as though all the anger that burst through her body was spilling out through the veins of them.

"Allura only has power as long as we feed it to her. Stop the flow of energy and it will cease to exist," Lily said out loud. Her voice was not wavering, she was strong, she would fight to the very end. "It's in our minds that we are giving this power to her. Stop it right now. Take back the control of your life. What kind of world do you want to live in?" Lily asked as she wished that they could see what she was seeing. How powerful they were in numbers, they had the strength together to overthrow any leader they wished, they just had to realize the truth. "Villagers of Praza, I know you are strong, you have powers that are far greater than this Queen on her own. Show your power," Lily yelled to the village folk, but to Lily's disappointment no one around Lily changed. They all stood still and stared.

"That's a wonderful little speech there, girl, but I'm afraid it's fallen on deaf ears. They do not wish your safety. Your comfort. I can give them everything," Allura interrupted, waving her hands over the people as though she owned them.

"You have a choice to stand with me or her. Who do you choose?" Lily yelled out again, still hopeful that the people would walk away from Allura, but they didn't. Their trauma was engraved deep within their minds, it wasn't simple to just leave.

Lily was disappointed as she watched the villagers stand still. And perhaps that was the most difficult lesson of all. The desire to help another when they didn't want her help. Seeing the future as being grim and not being able to do anything because others weren't willing to move past their differences. But still, Lily had made a commitment to try, and she would not stop yet. *Even if I am the only one setting the example, at least that meant one less person doing wrong in the world,* Lily thought.

"Enough childish nonsense!" Queen Allura yelled as the veins on her face strained from the anger in her heart. "She is one of them! Rain, I command you to pour!" Allura yelled, as she pointed to the large cloud that covered Lily. The cloud grew fierce, as the sound of thunder erupted and lightning bolted through the atmosphere. And as Queen Allura twisted her fingers above, the water fell down heavily completely soaking everyone in sight. But the magic around them did not cease, and a loud scream from within the crowd, disrupted the silence, revealing Oceana crying on the floor, only this time, her legs had disappeared and in replacement was a mermaid's tail.

"We have evil amongst us! Amongst our own people!" Queen Allura screamed as a loud roar of laughter cackled from her mouth. It poisoned her essence, and the pretty face that Lily once found appealing was replaced with an evil streak of madness that had overtaken her body. A black layer of smoke lifted from her feet, and as she moved closer to Oceana, it trailed behind in a dark shadow.

Oceana touched her tail hurriedly, trying desperately to dry it so that she could walk. But the water above from the cloud poured down too fiercely, soaking her skin and revealing her true self, as one with the water. Airlie quickly opened up her wings, trying to stop Allura from coming forward in a desperate attempt to save her sister. But it was no use, she was too small, and the water was too heavy, blocking her wings to fly properly. Allura clicked her fingers as two soldiers came forward, restraining both children. But now that Oceana was not covering her tail with her hands, the true madness could be seen, for there amongst the beautiful fins were small cut-out pieces removed from her fish tail, like someone had taken bites of her in small doses.

"What do we have here?" Allura peered over Oceana, examining the cut-out pieces. "Someone has been feasting for themselves and journeying for their own pleasure. Someone has been disobeying me!"

The crowd all looked to Marlina who was now breathing in short quick breaths and she looked down to the ground, embarrassed.

"You have been too greedy, too selfish," Allura said as she walked over to Marlina and pulled the orange necklace off her, smashing it into tiny pieces on the ground. "I gave you everything, and this is how you thank me?" Queen Allura's body jolted abruptly as her hair started to grow with extra length behind her. The long orange ponytail grew and grew and grew. Allura held the pieces of hair in her fingers, and then she hissed, cutting the hair from her head, and turning it into a long orange snake which slithered over to Marlina and wrapped itself around her body.

"My darling here is a bit hungry you see, she likes to eat naughty witches who disobey me. I'll let her squeeze you a bit first to give you some time to think about what you did," Allura said as she walked up closely to Marlina, watching with great pleasure as the snake continued to suffocate her slowly.

Lily was still safe inside her bubble but she didn't feel good about it. She wanted to help; she still wanted to save the people.

"The path to freedom is near," Lily yelled out. "You are all worthy of love, peace and happiness. Even you, Marlina. Redemption is available to everyone. The power of the universe is behind you. Can you feel it?" Lily said as she felt a strange buzzing sensation through her body. "Do not worry, she cannot harm you if you don't obey her. She is just one person shouting commands at you," Lily said as she pointed to Allura and she pulled out the smoke potion from the first land, Otor. The same potion to unleash one's authentic truth. She opened the lid and blew the smoke over the crowd. "Those who want to change, let us correct this wrong together. We need to not only release the stolen children, but we need to find the limiting belief within ourselves that tells you that you are unworthy of love. Dive deep within your mind to find where that idea originated from in the first place. We need to heal from the womb, let us journey together to the afterlife, and heal the ancestors from before!" Lily yelled out loudly as she then presented the potion that Devya had given her. "This requires no sacrifice. Imagine a protective bubble around you and take a sip of this. There is enough for everyone!" Lily rubbed her palm over the top of the jar and recited. "This jar is never-ending, let's share it together." Lily took a sip and handed it to the next person, and the next one after that.

"No!" screamed Allura as she pointed to her followers to take hold of the potion.

But to Lily's surprise, everyone in the village took a sip. The potion passed through every hand of every person that stood in front of her. Even Marlina managed for another to pour the potion into her mouth. Allura watched in shock as slowly her disciples were taking back their own power.

"Now, sit down, and let us call our Higher Self, our Spirit Guides, and the wisdom of the universe for protection," Lily said smiling with great relief as the villagers all followed her instructions.

Allura's eyes darted back and forth as she watched with horror her power being stolen from her in a quick flash. Even the tattoo-faced people who were Allura's loyal subjects had taken the potion, for they too were curious to see the enchantment of the foreign girl's actions. *Or perhaps they were addicted to the thrill of traveling to the afterlife,* Lily wondered. But then Lily thought to the words of wisdom she had learned along the way, that all creatures purely wanted to know love, to feel love and understand love, and here, Lily was giving them that chance to take love for themselves but this time, from themselves. That was the only kind of love that could never be taken away from them now.

"I call upon the rulers of Sa Neo. May you all bless us with strength," Lily said, as she envisioned those who ruled around her. As each King or Queen who carried the power of the land was called, they appeared around the circle as well.

The Najatinis presented themselves first, as Lily asked for help from her Higher Self. They encircled the villagers and held hands, in a protective circle, as they had done before with Lily. Their blue hair was pulled back tightly, twinkling stars on their faces, their gummy grin with few teeth, and they looked to Lily, excited, happy to see her. Devya appeared next, although not in the flesh. He was a flash of light; like the electrical currents that wove through his land, he appeared and disappeared. His spirit was flying over the villagers, guiding everyone safe passage on their journey to the afterlife. And the music from the Apprentices could be heard too, small beats of drums and songs of enchantment. Mia Veol's beauty could be felt as well. It washed over the people in a harmonious grace, bringing forth loving light, and strength. And lastly, even though Violetta would never be shown, Lily knew she was there, watching over them, and allowing such a profound movement of peace for future generations to come to take place.

Lily took a sip of the potion and closed her eyes too. Knowing her time to leave was coming near.

twenty-two

Ancestors

Lily drifted off into a deep sleep safe in her protective bubble, but when she arrived, the Middle World looked nothing like her journey with Devya. Lily was now standing upon a dirt road, and in front of her was a small illuminated light; it was showing a bonfire, with no flames. The wood and coals were burned up, and there was smoke coming from the ground. A group of spiritual souls were huddled around the fire, as though freezing, aching for warmth, yet the fire was not lit. And despite everyone's chill, no one was trying to light the flame. They were all staring at the empty darkness, angry, cold, shivering, and waiting for someone else to light their fire. Although they appeared to be outdoors, large windows floated past them. Behind each one was a beautiful scenario, a memory perhaps. One with sunshine, and desert hills, and camels. Another window was a garden with pink flowers and soft music. Another window floated by, this time it was a soft stream of water that trickled over little crystal stones. Each window held the portrayal of beauty, peace, and happiness. But the crowd of huddled people stayed staring at the empty fire, unable to move their vision elsewhere. The darkness of the energy was present, but Lily still felt her protective bubble encircling her, and the words of commanding her sacred space were stained in her memory. She had confidence, and courage to move through with her decision.

But the village people were nowhere to be seen. Their journey had taken them elsewhere. Still, Lily did not waver; she cleared her throat and spoke.

"I call upon the mother and father of Queen Jade and Allura. Make yourself present," Lily commanded, holding herself strong within her own spirit. Within moments, Lily could see two dark circles of energy moving toward her. And as they arrived, their bodies arrived too, a ghostly shell of misery. "And the grandparents of you too. And the generation before, and the one before that."

Several entities of floating light moved closer to Lily. They hovered in front of her, joining together and circling her.

"Now, I call upon everyone who is trapped here in this world. Those who are tormented by their own evil pathways and cannot move through."

Within moments, Lily was faced with a crowd of ten people: each parent had another parent who had passed on their own fear and misery. And it was an endless cycle of entrapment, of mind games, of an inability to feel self-worth or self-love standing before her. But the option to turn away was not possible. These souls were tortured, tormented, and weak. There was no evil strength before Lily, just a pile of sadness. The faces of the ghosts cried in misery. The energy was stale, and felt claustrophobic to be near, like they were in deep pain, wanting desperately to be saved.

"I am speaking on behalf of every creator, every living being, every breathing soul. We are sorry for what you went through. We know you did the best that you knew how to, and you lived your life according to what you thought was right. We are sorry for the wrong that was handed to you, and we heal those who have passed away, those who have left unjust behavior in their world. We are sending you love, and lightness, to move through this pain. To release the anger and misery you blame in this world. We are releasing the hurt, evil, and arrogance that you connect with your life here. We let go of everything that stops a flow of love and positive energy and remove toxic vibrations from the universe."

Lily used the ring on her finger to outline a circle as a door, like Devya did. And as she envisioned the door, it appeared, as a rustic wooden door with a great big golden handle. Lily reached forward and twisted the handle, allowing the door to open wide, and immediately a beautiful stream of bright light energy pierced through the opening, showing down on the ghostly souls below. The floating windows all stopped too, and immediately the ghosts all turned to see the miraculous imagery.

"Enter the light to move on and let go. Your story has been heard, your pain has been healed. You are forgiven, you have forgiven yourself. I am sending you love. I am giving you release. You are loved. You are worthy of a new beginning. Enter through the light and grace the next chapter of your entity."

The words Lily spoke moved through her body out of nowhere. She had no idea where they came from, nor where they were going. Yet Lily just allowed them to flow through her gently. She knew it was the voice of her Higher Self guiding her and speaking through her. Lily placed her hand on her heart and took a deep breath. She imagined a line of loving energy moving through her heart center and flooding to those ancestors in front of her. She was pushing love to those who had done wrong. And slowly, as the energy of love from Lily's heart center moved through the space, one by one, the ancestors walked through the opening of light. Some entered through the door, and others floated through the window. They continued to move until there were no more souls stuck in the space. The stars around Lily glistened more brightly now that the space had cleared around her, and she stared for several minutes, enamored in their delight.

"I am ready to return," Lily said, as she placed her hand on her heart, and closed her eyes.

But Lily didn't return, and instead, the sound of thunder broke through the silence, forcing her to open her eyes once more, and an electrical enchantment of bright lights filled the air. The atmosphere around Lily spun quickly. The lights shone in twinkling patterns, making her feel dizzy.

Lily's breath moved very slowly as she tried to regain consciousness despite the whirlwind of energy circulating. With one great exhale, the lights cleared, and the energy stopped moving. Lily was floating amongst the galaxy, surrounded in black nothingness. The moment that Lily surrendered her mind to try to understand what was happening was the second that a beam of white light, brighter than sunshine, glared from an opening up above, and it poured down onto her, flowing in an abundance like a waterfall. Lily had frozen in her position. She couldn't move. She couldn't look directly to the light, it was too bright to be seen. She closed her eyes and placed her hand on her heart, as she felt the energy of the spirit in front of her.

The feeling that surrounded Lily next was beyond comprehension. Lily didn't even want to try to understand it, because she felt that if she did, she would ruin the moment. It was a divine vibration of pure harmonic bliss, a nurturing warmth that radiated right to the core of her being. And so, Lily opened her heart to feel the blessing that was being given and upon doing so, clarity presented itself to her, as the memory of what was revealed itself. She was back inside her mother's womb, as a baby. A place of comfort, mysticism, and unlimited conscious energy. The feeling of nurturing love and safe support that she felt when she was inside her mother engulfed Lily's presence, and even though it was something she felt for only nine months, it was a feeling that she had carried with her throughout her life. And slowly, Lily opened her eyes again, realizing what was playing out before her. Tears from Lily's eyes wept down her cheek as she experienced a moment that she never thought she would ever feel in her life again. It was the feeling of her mother's presence so strong and so vivid that she realized that she had never even left Lily's side to begin with.

A humming sound of a sweet melody echoed through the air, and Lily felt at ease as the familiar sound of her mother's voice swam swiftly through her body. But Lily's mind switched to grief, as she had a glimpse of realization as to what was happening. And as the victimized child called out in her head, taking the reins over the tears flooding down her cheeks, she felt the courage to ask the question that burned her heart every time the name "mother" was uttered:

"Why did you leave me?"

The sound of an echo wafted through the air once more. But this time the words spoke clearly.

"It was not only my choice to leave you, Lily. It was yours too. We planned this together before both of us were ever born," she said, as the words danced in light energy, circling around Lily's body. "You wished to learn what a life would be like without a mother. You wanted to grow your strength alone. Even though I am not here, you have the same love surrounding you as ever before. For my love for you continues for an eternity, and my love supports you in every step of your way. Our love lives on in the unseen worlds."

The words from her mother nurtured Lily with harmonious grace. She felt as though she was listening to a dream, the way the words floated around her. And yet, the sounds of the vowels and every sentence that was spoken, Lily felt as though she had heard them before, for the knowingness that Lily's mother's love supported her was already engraved into her heart. But here, she was being reminded of that love, she was being shown the truth. Lily no longer needed to identify herself with the loss of her mother, she could instead rejoice for the gift of life.

"I love you," Lily said, as she closed her eyes and heard the same words reflect back inside her.

Lily felt the movement of energy flow through her body and swirl around her. And she lay there for several minutes, immersing her soul within her mother's vibration. Lily breathed slowly, noticing how gently her stomach rose as she inhaled, and the softness in her breath as she released it. Ever so gently, her breath encircled her heart, her body, and her mind. And as she breathed she realized that her mother's energy was always with her. It was entwined deep within her own heart so intensely that it was always part of her. For her mother had created this body for Lily to live in. It was her mother who allowed the manifestation of a miracle to take place, enabling Lily's soul to unite with her experience in life. It was not possible and would never be possible to lose that connection with her mother, for her energy lived on within Lily's heart. Lily smiled, as she allowed the blessings of the universe to bathe her, and with gratitude she exhaled, placed her hands on her heart, and opened her eyes.

twenty-three

In the Dreamtime

But when Lily opened her eyes, she was no longer standing on the world of Sa Neo. She was no longer floating between the unseen lands of the Middle or Upper worlds. She had returned to her real life with Papa in the beautiful mansion. She was sitting back home in her bedroom, in front of her dressing-table mirror, looking at her reflection.

The candle she had lit was still burning brightly in front of her, and the heat from the flame seemed to warm up the room, encircling a soft flickering where she sat. Lily had traveled through the worlds again, she knew it. And instead of fear of what had happened, she had a gleam of excitement. It was true: she traveled there; not only did she travel there, but she was able to control elements of it, as though the world she explored was a manifestation of her own projection. She dazzled with excitement, jumping up and dancing around in the same way the angelic creatures danced around the Wise Oak Tree. She knew this time that it wouldn't be long before she was to visit again.

Lily looked down to her hands. The amethyst ring sparkled on her finger, and her Ouroboros necklace was fastened tightly around her neck. Lily looked down to her body, to her arms and the clothes that she wore. If she squinted her eyes really tightly, she felt as though she could see for a second the glimpse of her Soul within her body. She could see the light projecting from inside her heart, through her body, and illuminating the space around her. And she thought about the energy that she held, how she now knew the secret to heal, and that something wonderful would soon be manifesting in its space. She placed her hand on her heart and closed her eyes. In a quick, solid heartbeat she felt as though she had moved into her heart center. Right in alignment with her Soul. And she smiled, knowing this was her new secret place. This was where she could fly free within herself, to be the best version of herself that she could be. It was here, inside of her all along.

Lily looked outside the window into the garden where her father was standing, cutting some red roses. She ran outside to meet him.

"Papa!" Lily yelled out as she joined her father near the rosebush.

"Hello, darling, it's stopped raining," he said as he rubbed her cheeks lightly. "Look at that beautiful rainbow."

Lily looked up to the sky. The heavy clouds had swept away, showcasing a beautiful beam of sunlight piercing through the atmosphere, and directly above where they stood, a huge rainbow shone through. Lily smiled from seeing such a miraculous delight. The sun warmed Lily's body up quickly, and it relaxed her mind as she breathed gently. She closed her eyes and tilted her head lightly up toward the sun, feeling the tingling sensation of sun-rays on her skin. The love from the sun reminded Lily of Sa Neo, and the beautiful presence of her mother by her side. It was true, the presence of her mother was absolutely everywhere.

"Did you know that your mother loved rainbows the most? She used to say that it was a gift from the angels, telling the world that they were looking over them."

"You never told me that papa." Lily smiled, hugging the side of his arm.

"Yes, I feel her near every time I see one." Father said as he looked at the rainbow and then looked to Lily.

"I feel her near always papa." Lily smiled back remembering so vividly the presence of her mother's words, energy and love shining within her.

"Here, smell this rose," Father said as he handed Lily a freshly cut rose.

As the edges of the uneven petals brushed across Lily's skin she breathed in the smell with utter delight. It was the familiarity of what she knew so well, the blessings of nature. And as she stared within the flower, she reflected upon the secrets of the universe. She felt as though the flower knew her every thought, the petals in front of her moved gently in line with her heartbeat. And Lily wondered, which was it that came first? Was her heart beating in accordance with the life of nature? Or was the flower moving in response to Lily's own vibration? Or was it neither? Were the flower and Lily moving together as one? Connected by a force so powerful, beyond either creation's comprehension, and together they floated peacefully, holding hands, in a sacred space of infinite time and divinity.

Phoebe Garnsworthy
About the Author

Phoebe Garnsworthy is an Australian female author who loves to discover magic in everyday life. She has traveled the world extensively, exploring Eastern and Western philosophies alike, while studying the influences that these beliefs have on humanity.

The intention of her writing is to encourage conscious living and unconditional love.

www.PhoebeGarnsworthy.com

www.LostNowhere.com

Other books by Phoebe Garnsworthy

Lost Nowhere: A Journey of Self-Discovery (Book 1 of 2)

Daily Rituals: Positive Affirmations to Attract Love, Happiness & Peace

The Spirit Guides: A Coming of Age Novella

Define Me / Divine Me : A Poetic Display of Affection

Printed in Great Britain
by Amazon